*Larify's Dismissal:*

*A Novel from the Hubbub*

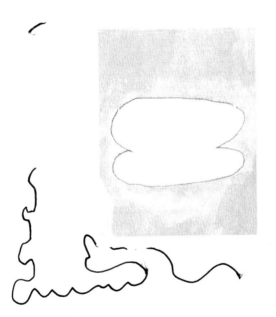

Nicholas the Poodle

*poodlepromise.com*

First Printed 2022


Copyright © Nicholas the Poodle Books 2022

ISBN 979-8-218-07680-1


Worcester, Massachusetts, USA

*Larify's Dismissal: A Novel from the Hubbub* is an original work and can be referenced with regard to its publication details.

Nicholas Dunphy

11/9/23

"An American is a complex of occasions, themselves a geometry of spatial nature –"

Charles Olson's *Maximus to Gloucester*
Letter 27 [withheld]

# Larify's Dismissal: A Novel from the Hubbub

**1.** The Bright Common

**2**. Blue Planet

**3.** Soapbox

**4.** The Water Company

**5**. Stop and Think

**6.** Limo

**7.** Days of the Tub

**8.** The Hairy Creature

**9.** Acorns

**10.** The Grass-Stained Astronaut

**11.** God in the US

**12.** The Merger

**13.** A Source

**14.** Bird Dogs

**15.** Birthdays

**16.** The Place in Deep Sleep

**17.** New Face

**18.** Building a Gravity Well

**19.** The Gift That Keeps On Giving

**20.** Coffee Talk

**21**. Larify's Passage

**22.** Newer York City

**23.** The Frumpy Blue Awning

**24.** High-Rise Family

**25**. Powwows

**26.** The Teacher's History of Robots

**27.** Letter in the Mail

**28.** Jeford, King of the Damned

**29.** Being Friendly

**30.** The Fashioner of a Saint

**31.** Last Legs

**32**. A Sea Lion's Red Ball

**33.** The Planet of Worms

## 1.  The Bright Common

Inside of a sun, made of light, creatures called *brights* mosey in a common that has buttressed ceilings. If one was to die, one could get the privilege to see the fantastic action within this star, 'though to die is relative,' as the resident spirits speculate. There are many things the brights think as they philosophize and lord over things called *ether wells*. These ether wells show continuous ages and lands in ether. It can be so lovely to see the ages the brights see. It is the brights who resemble people that like to collect patterns and motions they find through the ether wells, as the brights find stories and collect their favorites to keep in orbs. These brights let the orbs float into the vast catalogues in their star. Of what has happened in the universe so far, the brights only say, "Habijifus." In the bright common, there are other imitations of life, too. Peacocks, tigers, trees, and horses, these too are in the bright common and are brights also, made of the same stuff, light, but this light chooses to mimic animals or fauna and causes a rumpus in the common. Time, there is none in the Bright Common. The capable lights do not have a second – not a tick, nor a toc. They are always doing as they do. Yet there is a happening that distinguishes their existence. When one of the brights decides to live a life, the Common undergoes change.

In this novel, there is the story of a bright who decided to live a life and his name you shall be told.

It's gotten quite popular.

I think he is on the moon by now.

It began when an orb containing a revolution in France, with its peasant struggles, mass unrest, and the birth, reign, and exiles of Napoleon, was sailing under the common's rounded ceiling and a waddling bright tree paused to let the orb pass by. While doing so, a branch poked open a different orb, which let out its vapor, and that orb's story escaped to occur again.

Brights by the ether wells looked back at the perforated orb, knowing what was to come. An orb will break and be found again in the ether, perpetuated by its own eternity. Those playing overseers, the human-shaped brights, remained aside the ether wells unsurprised and said "Habijifus." Bright tigers leapt as the common's floor began to turn purple. The brights meshed together and then spread apart, sharing their emerald eyes, though one spark of light stood away from the blob by the common's rounded wall. From a passing orb, it noticed a whisp that showed a basket of heads aside a guillotine in a French square in 1794. This caused the bright to remember something powerful. This bright began to mutter,

"Crumbles,
Craters,
The pale light –
Red, white.
Oh yes, I must remind them.
It is the millennium.
I must live again."

The orb that had been opened contained a familiar age to the bright. It was the start of the 2000s in the United States of America. On high, a curvature of the common spread apart. An open space occurred. Through it, one could see the nearby thrashing of blue flares and the far-off stars. The bright flew to our moon, where it would dwell studying in a crater for many years. Alas, it returned, ready to live. When the bright landed on the common floor, there were two other brights waiting for it, as the story of one friend often requires other friends.

Larify is the name of the main bright.

There was another bright with yellow antennas lollygagging on the sides of its face and a pink back. This was Timjiffery, who also remembered what must be done. The third bright was Jeford. The bright common filled with red and a planet's symbol of the heart, so tiny hearts nearly covered the place, flowing up the walls into larger red hearts migrating in the common's dome.

All about, the brights looked down into the ether wells and concentrated on valiant events, like lanky oceans morphing into tributaries, or flowers awaiting bees, cold space, or people on tiptoes joining at the lips. Fine scents filled the common. Though, they could not be smelled by the brights. Brights are often forgetful too, so they forgot what was to come. Larify's old friend Jeford fluttered up to the dome. The bright pulled one heart out of the light, and this bright, Jeford, handed Larify what beats in my chest today as it beats in yours.

"Are you sure you want a heart?" Jeford asked.

"Life is a thankless labor," said Larify. "But I must go amidst the hubbub."

"You will be okay?"

"Better than that," said Larify, "I will be alive."

"Hmm."

Larify and Jeford were soon standing in a crevice in the bright common from which there illuminated a yellow light that permeated the star. Timjiffery handed Larify a rod, which the brights call a *world-flag*. With one, a bright can make their own world. A world-flag has the ability to change whatever the wielder sees to be a hinderance to their heaven. Larify held the world-flag in one hand and then placed the heart in his right breast. Timjiffery assisted him, making sure Larify switched the heart into his left breast. Larify went to the hole in the yellowing common's curve. There, he sat in a pale cart.

The cart teetered. A comet's tail streamed elsewhere, far in deep space. The cart soared forth. The hole behind the cart closed shut and the brights in their common remained deep in a shining sun.

## 2. Blue Planet


Timjiffery and Jeford followed Larify's cart through dark space in sight of distant suns. The process Larify would undergo to embody his life would be strange for a bright. As soon as one began to live, a bright would need to blend into an alien-folkway. Within the pale cart, Larify's ethereal form divided into pieces. These pieces ossified. Larify lay down as a human skeleton in the cart rushing through space. Timjiffery handed Larify books on biology and millennium politics, as well as several religious texts, which Larify skimmed then left floating. As the cart flew at three-times light speed, Timjiffery handed Larify purple skin. Larify stretched his purple skin over his skeleton. A nebula was visible in the distance. Blue nerves began to lace Larify's body, and he was starting to feel the thrill of beginning a new life.

A vast, blue heavenly body became visible. It was indifferent in its spinning like the brights had been in their heavenly doings. A majestic glow radiated from the planet. The bone cart did not yield, though as soon as it entered the ozone, the cart stopped short and Larify was flung into the planet Earth. Air surrounded him. Larify began gasping when soft lungs shaped in his ribcage. He had not yet gained weight, so his body slowed down in the sky. The ocean appeared to him. It became a flat cobalt blue until the varying currents and wrinkles of water were more visible. The tide was falling in some places while rising in others, but before he hit the ocean, Larify was saved as he landed on the prickly back of a housefly.

"Thank you, earthling," said Larify.

"Do not mention it," said the housefly.

Larify held onto his world-flag and his eyes scanned the ocean under his new blue eyebrows. Lowering closer to the water, the housefly flew forth at a steady rate while Jeford and Timjiffery flew at its sides. The two friends had become invisible.

After an hour or so, the fly inspected Larify using its tessellated emerald eyes. Then it said,

"I've got hard facts to tell you."

"Go ahead."

"First, your body is going to die, but you must feed it."

"Oh," said Larify, "I know that much."

"What else do you know?"

"I know about love and mystery and infinity."

A fertile, grassy coast was in sight. The fly let Larify off on a green ledge. The fly hated sappy things like Larify had said. The ledge rock was chalky, like moondust. There was a city nearby, but Larify did not think to go and visit and tell locals he was there to save the world, like Timjiffery suggested he do. Instead, Larify put his legs out before him and looked at his feet, and then he thought to himself, "I am here. I am in the mystery." Then he sang a song:

"I have opportunity
To be as I wish to be.
Maybe no one else can see.
My life will be of charity."

Before the night sky put away the sun to reveal the suns of other systems, the housefly returned.

"The second hard fact is all other things will leave you."

The fly spoke with its wings so the wings vibrated to give messages Larify could understand.

"Where are we going?" asked Jeford.

"The US," said Larify. "That's where the US people are."

The fly buzzed, then said,

"For another thing, *buzz*, the people of the US are rather dumb. Many fear deaths and cherish their own ignorance. They think it is wise to know little, but they are blinded by the little they know."

"That's why I came," said Larify, "I will tell all them it is the millennium."

"How old are you supposed to be?"

"I would like to be 17."

"Jesus," said the fly. "You cannot be 17, more like 32."

"Ah yes," said Timjiffery, appearing aside Larify with a scroll. "You see, Larify is an orphan from New Orleans…and now he is 32."

Timjiffery and Larify were pleased with this backstory.

"I have been a person many times," the housefly said. "It was after my last proper liberating incarnation that I had the chance to stop living all-together and dissipate into air, but I decided differently. Life is ugly but fun to me," said the fly. "See, in my tongue we had a saying, 'to be as a fly on the wall.' I became fascinated by this. *Buzz*. I reasoned in my last body that it was truly impossible to understand what another person's world is like outside of my own senses. I wanted to be with people in their private moments. I wanted to see what it was like when others were alone. So, I became this – a fly. Though I have abilities. Naturally, a housefly like me only lives a couple weeks, while I live as long as I want, and I can change sizes, as you see now. *Buzz*. We ought to shrink down while it's light. You don't want to barge in on the world of people like this. You're riding on a fly. They may kill you. Records show people kill what they don't instantly understand."

The housefly spoke again:

"We will be at the East Coast in a day's time. I will put you in New York City, where many things begin. *Buzz*."

"Okay," said Larify, who felt happy to see the sun rising at the end of the tide.

"Be careful Larify. I will be here for you, but don't be too surprising."

"…"

"You know there are human ways of doing things, right?"

"Yes, sure."

"Most like you to be kind and all, but don't make a show of it."

"Okay."

"Blend in," said the housefly.

"They will like me as I am, I think," said Larify.

"Likely not," said the fly.

So the housefly and Larify both shrunk.

Later, the fly itself became perturbed by the wind. Larify did not ask to rest on the dimly lit coast or any buoy so his carrier flew on through the day and night. The bright was happy to learn new things, so he peered into the darkest spots of the ocean. He began to feel the coldness of the wind and the clicking teeth that trembled under his lips. The blood retreated from Larify's newly formed toes and fingers. Larify felt ever proud of the man he was becoming. This feeling overtook his cold body as the sky was brightened again by the sun peeking over the tide's end. Jeford and Timjiffery continued to glide alongside the housefly. Larify listened to the wind.

Eons ago, the ocean had wrapped this planet, remaining on lands for rivers and streams and lakes. Larify's approximate air was comfortable. He dared not to think too hard about the ocean. Larify closed his eyes. While his body soared through the light blue sky, he saw the Bright Common from above in his mind's eye, where brights stood over ether wells. The Bright Common would always be his first memory. He opened his eyes. Ocean water went underneath his view. Sand was dancing beneath the surface, passing through sunbeams in the green depths. Larify was very excited. The housefly buzzed a grunt as Larify was getting heavier and more lifelike.

Seaweed, sticks, and other signs of land were showing up on the tide. This happened as the sun set again. The evening turned purple, and the sound of churning waves seemed louder while the cold made Larify shiver. The whole while, Jeford had been soaring beside the housefly as a sparkle and he began to wonder 'Will I ever live?' 'What will the US have for a bright like me?' Jeford flew at Larify's left and Timjiffery stayed at his right, and then Timjiffery flew ahead to inspect the East Coast that was coming into view. The statue of liberty was before the distant cityscape. A shadow fell from the oxidized copper statue. It glided over the depths, approaching the housefly. All of a sudden, the shadow animated a mass of ocean water and Larify beheld a leviathan with a puffy head and big boobs. Mist surrounded its face. The entity raised its hand and waved Larify closer.

"Go on," said the bright.

The fly did as Larify asked, flying closer to the mist as its legs dangled.

"You are approaching the land of the free," said the shadow. "I am here to welcome you."

"Thank you," said Larify.

"..."

"Hello."

"Hello," echoed the shadow of liberty. "You will soon touch busy streets. I am the liberty to choose. I may show myself in many forms but remember this Larify: freedom comes with choice."

"..."

"No matter what you see, remember why *you* chose to live."

The shadow of liberty then collapsed to the ocean. The shadow moved westward like the shadow of a plane on water and stayed behind the statue of liberty. Larify heeded the eerie advice. "No matter what you see, remember why *you* chose to live." Then Timjiffery came, carrying a leather rectangle.

"This is a wallet," Timjiffery explained. The brights inspected the various cards and Timjiffery provided his best explanation for the function of each card. Timjiffery handed Larify two blue credit cards. When Larify passed the wallet to Jeford, his bright friend did not take it, so the leather rectangle fell. The wallet twirled to the ocean then sank in hours to a seabed.

On the housefly, Larify approached New York City by night and went aside the statue of liberty that stood with its cold torch. Inside the statue, glowing souls of immigrants marched on a spiral staircase. Streetlamps reflected off the water near the waterwall of the city proper. The fly flew low near the water and zipped up to a railing, letting Larify onto the sidewalk. Larify walked several feet buck naked. The bright assumed the average height of a man. Timjiffery appeared and gave him a coat and comfy cotton pants. This clothing was found in a garbage bag beside the steel container of a certain charity. Glass windows were firm on the building-sides. A median of grass was between the water and the buildings. Apartments had spots of light like some foggy homage to dalmatians. The street bent to the right of an aquamarine storage facility, and though Larify minded this direction, he found his feet carrying him forward along the coastline. Larify kept one hand on the waterwall's railing while planting his world-flag into the ground with his other hand.

A man was playing a tuba.

A bookshop was closed indefinitely.

A grill in front of a ghetto shop sizzled. There was constant babble. 'If only the stars could see this,' Larify thought to himself, surrounded by action and unintentionally stopping as his skull gawked at the sign for Canal Street. There bodies of all sorts – trees, people, rats, the hazes in the muddled space under the sky – were in a hubbub. Larify was eyeing all the bodies and thinking, 'Look, that's me,' 'Look, that's me,' 'Look, that's me.'

That night, the bright found himself in a huddle of park people who questioned him. They did not ask him things so much as said things aloud to see if he were phased. Larify smiled and nodded and he shared a blanket with a woman beside a tree. As sunlight combed the grass to prepare it for the next day, Larify was visited by a bright who stepped off a sunbeam just to say, "Hello." Daylight ghosts smoked cigarettes on the building terraces. Larify was quite energized by his own antics, as he was alive and in the city. From the park conversations he overheard, Larify understood he had to get to the DMV. There he could get an identification card.

As he walked through New York City, he saw Americans around him bustling, chatting, or moving in familiar lines to workplaces or homes. Larify found the DMV all on his own without help from the housefly, Timjiffery, or Jeford. There were people standing outside of the front. "The DMV is dull and awful," he was told, so it became so. Hundreds of seats were under the low ceiling inside. People stood up tapping their feet or sat in empty spaces. It was rather bright in there, and he watched the changing occupants on sheen chestnut benches. A voice kept announcing numbers that appeared in red dots on a thing. It took Larify a few moments to realize he had to take a placeholder. He waited for a half-hour. Abruptly, a perturbed old fellow said, "I hate waiting." Larify could not change waiting with this world-flag though. He had to wait, too. When Larify's number came, (it was 44A), he went to the counter and told the woman he needed an identification card.

"I'm from New Orleans," he said. "I'm 32 years old."

Larify did not have the proper documentation so he was sent away.

He went outside and sat on the ground.

A group of young men in scaly caps approached him and assumed he was an old drunk because of the color of his face.

Larify learned from this group of pseudo-Irish that he could get a fake ID on the Internet. The pseudo-Irish are descendants of Irish in America who call themselves Irish though are only partly so and are generations removed from the immigrants but dress as if every day is St. Patrick's Day. Larify looked at a computer for a while in an internet café, but he did not have a screenname, nor any information to provide in the empty rectangular boxes on the websites the internet could reach. He returned to the pseudo-Irish, who were then sitting at a high table outside of Duffy's Tavern, and they told him fake IDs were made in Japan.

So Larify went to the waterwall's railing, waited till night came, and then he boarded the housefly again.

In route to Japan, the fly said,

"Larify, I love what you're doing, but you need to get by like a man. *Buzz*. Isn't that why you are here? *Buzz*. There is this saying, 'Grow up.' It's supposed to mean that people get closer to death, get over their petty thinking, and see the source of light for the world, but more commonly it means to withdraw immediately from questioning things and pretend like you know what's going on."

"Well, first he needs a self to grow," said Timjiffery.

The fly buzzed on in the darkness.

"That's why he needs an ID. That's what they do in the world. If you have a self, you have an ID for it."

Far behind the group, back in New York City, a creature gargling long empty nothings and lying its best to keep things in order, sneered. Its alabaster frame glinted in the moonlight. A shadow was cast over near building tops. Off Larify went, happy to be soaring on the housefly with his world-flag, not yet aware of that alabaster monster called Bureaucracy.

The world filled with things, names, and rules.

## 3. <u>Soapbox</u>

Obtaining an ID card somewhere in the Far East was the goal of the party. The brights admired ocean liners and cruise ships on the tide. After flying toward the European continent for hours, the housefly realized a safer direction and turned around. It turned 180 degrees & trailed the sun. It stayed just minutes before the sunline. Larify watched the US below turn from city to forest to prairie.

The world took time to cover, for sure.

Twice the fly landed as Larify requested they visit a 24-hour diner. Larify got used to plucking things like green sprouts, beans, kielbasa, and toasty bread with a fork then chewing. He was using monies Timjiffery and Jeford found on the sidewalks and under old tattered cushions. The brights took coins from the pans of the people collecting money from the people waiting for a red light to turn green in an intersection. Enjoying his diner grub much, Larify shared it with the fly, which would shrink to normal housefly size and feed on Larify's plate. Plenty of space was left to Larify by waiters and diner patrons. He had been in the world for three days without a shower. Larify was stinky, snot-nosed, and repulsive. He gently patted the back of a fly, which, unbeknownst to the rest, winged things like, "You ought to clean yourself up Larify. Remember, appearances mean too much to the lot here." The lack of hygiene was somewhat encouraged by a certain college student. Early one morning, she confided in Larify at a diner. The student told him he was lucky to be ugly because people would leave him alone.

He told her, "It's the peaceful millennium, you know."

Coloring the world in light, the sun illuminated a city on the coast of Japan that Larify saw after flying for half a week. Cliffs with blue rocks loomed. Having done reconnaissance on the land, Jeford and Timjiffery flew from the cliffs toward the housefly who buzzed a grunt when it noticed.

"You must see Tokyo," said Timjiffery.

"I remember that name," said Larify. "I saw it in an atlas."

"Yes, but you must see it. There, it is always the future!"

"I love it," said Jeford. "When I live, I want to live in Tokyo."

"Buzz," said the fly.

After spending a few days in the city ogling, Larify took time to shower and soak in a hotel. He drank from a teacup and smiled like a goon at the sunrise. Then he saw the shadow of liberty in his sink. "...Remember why you chose to live," he remembered. He had to move. Larify, who spoke Japanese, began to ask around a marketplace where he might find the means for identification, saying he lost his own. He was standing in a busy stall, chewing meat off a stick with the fly on his shoulder when he happened to chat with a man wearing a tarboosh. The man had skimpy facial hair and a kind, puffy face. It turned out this man could help. Larify followed this person to a nightclub, which was entered through a door covered in flyers beneath a gymnasium. Marching through a hallway past paraphernalia in black light, the club owner said, "I don't care a trifle for the rules of the world," and he soon opened a curtain, revealing his ID printing operation. The fake IDs he made were top notch and had the necessary holographic. Larify could get a fake passport, too. The nightclub had all sorts of US paraphernalia, like likenesses.

When Larify mentioned that he was going to "Awaken the world," the man clarified what Larify meant, and then, pinching hair on his chin, the club owner remarked that the US "...can never awaken until it wants peace more than personal gain." Larify repeated this aloud to understand better, "...peace more than personal gain." He watched the club owner alter a digital template and scale the picture of Larify's face, a face that had recently been doused in fine shampoo, and soon Larify was standing outdoors in Japan with identification.

Larify wondered if in time the US would right itself and avoid mishandling the millennium's start by perpetuating the peace instead of media, and he continued to think as he checked out of his room, only to notice he had moved when he keyed in on a goldfish going *glub glub* in a bowl behind the concierge's desk. The goldfish was regurgitating the bowl's pebbles. The concierge left his hand on the desk upturned as he waited for Larify to reclaim his ID card and passport, which Larify finally presented after having made excuses. The bright was not yet used to carrying extra things. His mighty world-flag had been minimized into a lapel pin that he kept in his breast pocket. Timjiffery had stolen Larify a lavender button-up shirt from a flea market.

During their next stretch of flying, the housefly seemed to be growing disappointed in Larify's progress. He was not getting around himself. The fly was telling him "hurry up" and "stop looking around so much at random things." "If you do not make haste soon," the housefly warned, "you will never get to a place where people truly love you." The fly was making references increasingly often to a specific regret in its own past life, this one regret involving a love of the fly's.

"Surely she is growing old alone again without me," the fly whined.

As they flew over Asia toward the US, Larify saw Death as a transient black shape over a Chinese forest. They glared at one another, Larify and Death. With pincers for hands, the dark abstraction motioned for Larify to close his eyes and cradle his head back and forth to sleep eternal slumber. Larify took out his world-flag and aimed it. He considered making a change. Larify had seen from the moon how fear of death made people dysfunctional and death itself caused loss, but on second thought, Larify found he would never return to the Bright Common before dying, nor would his hair grow or harsh moments end ever, so he was unsure if it was wise to erase Death. Death remained watching Larify soar on the housefly's back.

It stood high above the trees. Birds were flying round its shoulders.

By the time they reached Europe, Larify was thinking that the US surely had a lot of military bases all over the world.

Distracted from Larify, the housefly landed.

Sorry to relate, but the fly had let the bitterness of a funk preoccupy it.

Setting Larify down on the Aegean island of Patmos, the housefly took off to do "Errands, *buzz*." Larify's stomach was full, and he had bought a useful traveling cloak. He came upon a stable that amounted to wooden beams on a grassy plateau and was nondescript at the base of the hills. The stable was with horses. Larify tried to preserve his clean cloak as he lay down to sleep that night in the stable. The ocean was surging over the cliffs and Larify could hear it in his ears until he fell asleep. The next day, the sun rose. Hours of anticipation strained Larify's mind, but this did not move him any nearer to fixing the shortsightedness of the US because the fly never did return to bring him anywhere, and then, at dusk, a tall ghost walked into the stable.

Larify's shirt was over his nose, for he was trying to interview flies about his housefly pal while they swarmed a pile of horse poop. The ghost looked at Larify and Larify looked to see the teeth of a glowing old man.

"Hullo Sojourner," said the ghost. "You're a bright, I presume."

There was familiarity between the two, as if they had met before.

Then the ghost said,

"Come – let's drink hot water."

Larify had to think for a second, then he sat up, patted his hair, and shook out his leg. The ghost led Larify out of the stable to his shelter, which was nearby. The man calmly placed a table between the two of them. Then he heated a kettle full of water.

Larify sat down on a three-legged stool.

"I am so glad you can see me," said the stranger.

"I have eyes," Larify noted, "how couldn't I?"

"I am a poet….and I am a ghost," the tall man explained, making his own eyes large. "I died in the year 2000 exactly."

"…"

"By God, may I ask – are you trying to do good in the world?"

"Yes, in the United States," said Larify. "I want US people to know that it is the promised millennium of peace and they can relax and let God take over the world."

"Ah," said the ghost. "My name is Robert Lax. I am from New York myself, but you really needn't know that about the US. I was quiet in my time. I knew my own place."

"…"

"You look as if you want to find yours, Larify. Am I right?"

"I know mine," said Larify.

"Mm."

"I exist. I am pure of heart."

"Tough to do both, but do do it," said the arch poet critic.

A rock flew into the shelter.

A slit opened in the rock, and it began to explain:

"People in the US are miseducated. Having assumed they've been there for several generations, they do not find the old ways of humankind, and they make importance out of such…panicked things. That is of course my gross generalization. It is a common one dressed up in different ways. It was not my excuse though. You can find real free thinkers in the US. I recommend destitute individuals. There are scholars and beats. People work overnight in convenience stores. As for me, I mostly stay here on Patmos. Though my body is in Olean."

A 'paillasse,' which is a straw mattress, awaited Larify against the wall of the room. When he dreamed, he was back in the Bright Common, free, springing about on all fours with a bright leopard through dancing bright trees. Larify woke up feeling amused. He saw his purple legs. Larify noticed the shelter was empty. He went outside. He could faintly make out the ghost of Robert Lax standing on the cliff, looking at the sunrise. Robert Lax turned to Larify and motioned to him with his hand. Soon the ghost led Larify to a dinghy.

"I used this myself long ago," said Lax.

Larify settled into the hull, crouching down carefully. He felt for the balance he would need while in the boat. Looking down at Larify, the ghost of Robert Lax told him, "…remember Larify, they may know you love God but cannot know why."

Larify took up the two oars and patted the water dumbly, then the ghost pushed the oars with arms that stretched.

Robert Lax said,

"row, row, row"

"row, row, row"

"row, row, row"

Larify got this stuck in his memory as he pushed out into the water. The cadence was helpful long after he could no longer see Robert Lax. Why should I tell you of Larify's strains in the turquoise tides of the Aegean Sea when all there was to do for days was row, row, and row? He had to motivate himself. But Larify was supported by his sheer brawn and not knowing a way otherwise, the labor was immense. As a new man, Larify's dedication was primal. It was the type only executed by one who is sure he will have some point in the world, pausing never to be taught he is puny in comparison to the waters surrounding him, and Larify was too naïve to go onto land and take some more technological transport, as the dinghy pleased him well enough. Knowing he was alive and would never give up, Larify's fervor for rowing grew like the puddle of saltwater that pooled around his ankles at the bottom of his boat. Larify slept one night stock-still in the wooden boat, only to awaken by moonlight and continue rowing despite the lack of an apt direction.

The marvelous Aegean Sea was graced by leaping dolphins at moments that made Larify thrilled. Larify rowed and rowed in search of the world he could make better. By the time Larify was passing through the strait of Gibraltar, the canal between Spain and Morocco, he felt zealous, but also sunburned, noticing his own reddened feet and salt covered gut. The sea transmitted to rivers and joined its blue to the blue of the Atlantic Ocean, and the waters of the world wrapped the planet's shape like a Christmas bauble. Billions of people woke and slept and lived in their private cubits of personal space, no more special than the ripples in the tide.

The dinghy had taken in crabs and fish that Larify ate like a badger. From the air, there came a magpie. Larify recognized the species by the midnight blue tips on its wings. Larify knew it was a British magpie from his studies on the moon. 'So how is it so far South?' he wondered. The magpie was big and made partly of metal, and all of a sudden, this bird plucked Larify's passport from his cloak pocket and flew up into the air. Reactively, Larify aimed his world-flag and produced a gossamer that lassoed the magpie. He held on as the bionic magpie dragged his boat for two days, but due to exhaustion he fell asleep. When Larify woke up, he was wrapped in a towel. A bare room surrounded him. It was concrete and powder blue with only a steel table and an examiner. A Scotsman was asking him questions about his identification. Larify remembered he had a bottom lip. He wagged his head around like a ball. The policeman was holding the world-flag. By then the tool resembled a mere walking stick. Larify, whose face was covered in sea salt, lurched forward. When he hollered, "I'm alive! I'm alive!" the Scotsman beat him down.

Larify was put in a hold. The bright, still ecstatic to be human, was stripped naked, his cavities were checked, and he was given scratchy sweatpants and a bologna sandwich. Larify's voice returned after a juice box and a spare juice box his cell mate did not want. At a table, the Scotsman checked Larify's fake ID card. He was fooled by the holographics. He saw that Larify was from New Orleans.

Weeks before, Larify had had his 32nd birthday on October 20th.

When asked about his passport, Larify said, "A bird took it." A guard nodded and repeated this to other guards in the office.

At night, Larify looked out from the window of his cell. The small window was one of forty windows on the side of an ugly brick penitentiary. As he was focusing on a few pine trees, Timjiffery appeared outside the window.

"Larify! Are you okay?" asked his friend.

"Yes, I think this is part of my life," said Larify.

"I think so too."

Timjiffery flew toward the stars.

There was a full moon, radiant behind trafficking clouds. The silvery light gave Larify the feeling of nostalgia, like when even the dullest of mortal minds feel life is merely swinging their eyes in some eternity. While Larify was feeling optimistic, his cellmate roared then coughed and growled. The prisoner crouched by the toilet. His scratchy jumpsuit ripped. The tares filled with wolf hair. Guards came in and threw themselves at the changeling. Larify watched and pouted his lips as they beat his dehumanized cellmate. The brown man was tased and fell to the floor and into an unconsciousness dream world.

The next morning, it was explained to Larify in the jail lobby that he was being let out so long as he did not mention anything about people turning into wolves in their jail, so Larify took his bag of clothes, his world-flag, and boarded a bus to Edinburgh's old town. He was in a courtyard having breakfast outside the Castle Café when the magpie that had stolen his passport was spotted atop a thin chimney. Larify glared as the bionic magpie dropped his passport to the cobblestones.

That day, Larify felt embarrassment for the first time. He had just started to exist and yet he was considered a 'prisoner,' and it got worse. As he walked up the Royal Mile, he saw, on a digital tablet, the image of his body on the sands of a beach, and on a cellphone, this image was reposted on another digital forum where profiles were adding captions, and so Larify's misfortune was being turned into a meme.

He could not tell if the words in the comments were by people or the Internet, so he backtracked to rub the golden toe of David Hume, an eminent philosopher with a statue on the royal mile. Edinburgh's university students rub this golden toe for good luck before tests. This day had certainly happened before, but Larify felt incapable by the nighttime, like he had made some mistake. Using ears, Larify took in the evening dinners with their tinkling glasses and huffy exchanges. Intimate tables could be seen through plate glass. A young waitress in tight pants left a pub after her shift. Mothers and fathers walked toward homesteads. Loners paused on the raised sidewalks of Edinburgh beside the damp stone tenements, and Larify, with his own ears, heard the magnetic buskers, and the unhurried considerations of souvenir shoppers. Larify saw all the bright objects being very human, caught in some foreign earthly beauty.

So many of the people seemed to belong there in the city. Larify looked to the sun sinking in the distance of a navy-blue sky. He himself was not yet accustomed to the star where human souls float after life.

He felt embarrassed about his inability to understand the civic laws at hand.

He sat beside an enclosed tree.

'What is the act of loving?' he wondered. 'Do I have to go out and touch things to show I love?'

Larify then continued to poke about all night. Tempting women, some of whom were done up in make-up that made their faces yellowish, shook their hips on the cobblestones, and when the area was empty, he passed St. Giles Cathedral. Larify looked aside him to another statue, this the statue of an economist named Adam Smith. Smith was ten feet tall with his right hand on a globe. He stood by as the Cathedral rose up to a dark heaven aside him. Larify could see groups of hooligans and mates exit stag parties.

"Trinkets and baubles!" the statue exclaimed.

Larify and Adam looked at one another.

"What irks me," said the statue, "is that I worked very hard until I died. I thought of morality, and I thought of free-market trade. I told the formula of capitalism in detail, but I also told the people to avoid the purchase of frivolous trinkets and baubles. Now I see the yankees buying a hundred pairs of shoes! Isn't it incredible how beings work the world into monumental ideas, only to die and leave generations living in their ideas, unaware? It is like the creation of a trance."

"Ah."

"What's your name?"

"Larify."

"Are you Scottish?"

"No."

22

"I published *The Wealth of Nations* in 1776, the same year they signed their Declaration of Independence."

Larify explained that he did not know that. Economics was not his forte.

"That is no excuse to ignore recent history!" scolded Adam Smith.

"…"

"You know," said the green mouth of Adam Smith's statue, "whenever I had a taxing idea, I would walk about all night until I found myself in some far-off pasture, frozen, as the light came over the end of the land."

"I like walks, too."

Larify tapped a cobblestone with his world-flag.

"What about the *impartial spectator*. Have you heard that one? My idea that to judge morality one would need a neutral, indifferent observer to observe and pass fair judgement."

"I thought that was my idea."

"Christ, Larify."

Larify explained that he only knew it was the millennium. A time in human history when there would be heaven on Earth. If Adam Smith could have moved his arm, he might have touched his green, oxidized chin with his hand. Adam Smith shouted to the statue of David Hume, "Hey Hume! This one is repeating a rather bonnie scooby!" It was strange to see, not just because it was a statue shouting, but because the statue was yelling to another statue many meters behind his head. David Hume heard. The empiricist grimaced then nodded, continuing to stare down the nearby bridge.

'It's not just an idea,' Larify thought.

"Okay," said the arch economist Adam Smith. "I am going to help this operation, but you must heed my tenant."

"Yes?"

"If you don't know the ideas that keep humans in bubbles you will never get out of bubbles!"

"Bubbles. Okay."

"I want you, sir, to be like *the invisible hand* that was supposed to manage global wealth. Have my secret fortune. It will start you off. Within the Canongate Kirkyard yonder, before a decorated wall, you will find the grave of my body. If you hold your hand on the inscription until sunrise, bricks of gold will appear at your feet as the sun rises."

Adam Smith's statue kept talking about the mishandling of his ideas and Larify walked down the mile to the graveyard, over the lawn, and to the grave of Adam Smith. He pressed his hand against the inscription and waited in the cold cemetery until sunrise. The gold bricks started to appear as light on the gravel. Then, at Larify's feet, there was heavy gold. Larify took his hand from the wall and picked the gold into his arms, and traveling toward him in the morning sky, there came an orange flame.

It had been sent from the Statue of Liberty's torch.

The mock-flame landed and Larify climbed into its doorway to sit on a little bench. Then the flame went back into the sky and headed west, showing Larify cliffs and taking him swiftly over the ocean. The flame twirled toward New York City. In ten hours, it reset in the statue's torch. Larify swam to the city. Passing through the streets, he entered into a square. He looked up at the digital displays. One had a pink cherry logo.

It read,

[We are trying to look moral and necessary for you to buy our product. Though we do not know you, we can front like we do. Our computerized research studies your behavior like the behavior of chimps. We don't give a damn about you, really. How could we? Since we have never met you, we only assure you *you* are who needs our trinkets and baubles.

Now, buy our gear and help us get bigger for we have convinced ourselves we have something interesting enough and all our employees work for money.]

Larify said, "At least the ads are honest."

"No," said Timjiffery, who flew to Larify's right. "Right now, you are able to see what is meant versus what it shown to the public. Hold on to this Larify. Great change is ahead."

Larify gave Timjiffery his bricks of gold to invest. He then walked to Manhattan and into Central Park. There the fields were yellow, and the people were sheepishly watching the park. Larify climbed on top of an old soapbox.

"The country is young, but spirit is old and learned!" he said. "It is the millennium. A thousand years of peace is upon us!"

Larify's outcry brought many phone cameras, but it was because he was odd looking. The people did not understand his story about a housefly, nor had they read anything from *The Wealth of Nations*. Protestors with cardboard came. On some of the cardboards there were crucifixes. Larify's hair was getting long and he was wearing a cloak. In the US, if you have long hair and a bright spirit, people think you think you are Jesus because they themselves are afraid to meet their maker.

The giant of Bureaucracy loomed.

### 4.  The Water Company


Next, Larify did hairbrained human stuff. Spreading his influence throughout the United States, Larify rented 10 offices, invested in businesses, then sponsored 100 charities. The bright paid workers in Alabama to carry urns, scoop brown water out of the Mississippi and ship the river water to certain US cities. The *Larify.co* teams put the water into large vats. Blue dye was mixed in certain vats and *Larify.co* dyed downtown districts and residential areas blue. All over the country, things were bluer. His world was becoming the popular one to many. In passing cars, Larify heard people of the US listening to his favorite music like Circa Survive and Blue Oyster Cult. The public became "blue with things," meaning they dressed in blue. It was as if Larify invented a color. Ads for *Larify.co* appeared in major cities. Across the Internet, there flashed a window with Larify's smiling face, saying, "I am from an odd star system..." The people started to jest, "I am from an odd star system, too." Being so popular, many things he thought became niche companies. One result of *Larify.co*, for instance, was a movement that put small fireplaces in the gutters for those who lived in sewer sludge – another result was an expedition to the planet Mercury – and Larify outlawed paper straws. His company *Larify.co* grossed ten million dollars in three years, and then he monopolized water. *Larify.co* then made fifty million dollars. In the meantime, Larify had sex with 1,000 women.

Big data collected opinions about Larify.

Of his efforts, some started to say, "Larify is stupid," though he thought earlier not to be so.

'One can never do enough good,' Larify realized.

The bright was meshing with the public, and though he was very capable, Larify did not know what exactly to change with his world-flag and decided to let people have Earth as it is. Larify started to give away more of his money. He was putting things on the Internet himself and he refused to believe things on the Internet are the things they show because of the *Tractatus Logico-Philosophicus*, which was first published in 1921. Larify then made another five million dollars. Whenever he needed emergency loot, he would ask Timjiffery or Jeford to collect coins or steal and pawn. One day, the brights robbed everybody walking around in Boston. Then Larify decided he knew what to do next; he was going to make a one hundred dollar fine for moving past age-old, universally valid statements just to speak. This may slow what the bickering people bickered to him about. He was 37 by then, and life had accelerated with many phone calls and dates. Larify had to battle many unfocused conversations and though he always reminded others, "It is the peaceful millennium," this seemed to be a least interesting aspect of his company. So, to assert this fine, Larify marched on to the Blue Hills in Boston and he asked Lancaster the Politic to implement the fine for idle chatter. The Politic was a ridge of ice atop a hill, then covered in fallen brown and orange leaves. Larify had no idea what to do when he got there, for the Politic had no face and nothing at all to say. The ridge of ice just remained there with the name, 'Lancaster the Politic,' carved into it, and one day the ridge of ice would melt.

## 5. Stop and Think

As Larify's mission progressed, he started to reflect on his life while taking a bath. It was the millennium, certainly, and he was doing well. But were other people well? Larify saw all the messages on the Internet, his brand, his face, his name, but Larify considered, 'What if I am just a naked body in a bathtub?' and 'What if the planet I am on would not change one bit had I not lived?' and finally he wondered, 'How can I be just about money?' Then Larify gave two million dollars away. He took a video. He went to a hotel he owned. He walked in and raised his hand to be shaken, as they do on Earth. Some became excited by the sight of him. Larify rode the elevator to his private super-suite, ran hot water through miraculous indoor plumbing, then put himself in another bathtub. He rested for two hours, closing his eyes. In the blue bath water, he was a shrine in a pond. Though he was in a hotel. Larify never really spoke to anyone while he gave people what they asked for. And Larify was lying and soaking. Epsom salt had been sprinkled into the water, but he did not fall asleep. All of a sudden, Larify noticed something about himself – he had spent millions of his dollars on the work of painter Jean-Michele Basquiat, and as the sunlight reflected on a brown painting, he saw the letters 'L – A – R.' He realized his name was there in the paint, among the scattered letters. Larify began to think of his use again. He thought of a cockamamie unconditional idea, like 'What if big things are just as necessary as little things, like the hairs on my epidermis?' He walked out of the tub naked, looked at the painting, went to the window and thought, 'So what do I get rid of?'

He had a breakdown.

Days went on and dollars were passed.

The blue cards inserted.

Judging by the behavior of US people, all things were working if they got the money that day. But this was every single day.

Larify spent time cracking acorns underfoot.

Then one day, as he was standing around at 12 in the afternoon with nothing to do, he bought more paintings of Jean-Michele Basquiat at a gallery. Docents sneered at his tall jacket collar that accentuated his purple chin. It was a collar with a dorsal curve by his cheek. People would see it and remember wild boars. This was fashion. Then they muttered this was Larify of *Larify.co* and he was a big, flashing hit. Larify then spent ten million dollars on more works of Jean-Michele. He had a collection going. Many paintings were walled at his Californian abode. In a tub he sat, one November day. By this point, the Internet did not like Larify, and Larify did not love the Internet. As a matter of fact, he could not believe how the Internet was very unlike him alive in a room.

## 6. <u>Limo</u>

Larify bought a pasture of deer in Boston. Certain women popped into Larify's head for each moment he was sorry for not being able to marry them and be their one & only, and while Larify was reminiscing one morning, he sensed there was a large presence three floors higher. The presence was heavy and buzzing. Larify went onto the roof, up through one of his corporate super studios near Back Bay in Boston. The housefly met him atop one of the many *Larify.co* buildings. The underside of the housefly was broad, and the fly retreated slowly (for itself) in the air.

Then the housefly called to Larify,

"I have returned!"

"Hello," called Larify.

"You did not look for me!" the housefly scorned.

"Well, if you are an immortal soul doing figure eights, flying about the world, picking me up and advising me, you will be okay, I figure."

"Balls," said the fly.

"Plus, I told you. It is the millennium."

"No, this cannot be it," said the fly. "You are a liar.

Because the star is quiet

I told you what it says,

But now I am your enemy.

Thanks to you, I must live again.

After

I will make life for everyone around you *hell*!

And it will be your fault."

Larify downplayed this and smiled and turned down his hand.

He could not understand the fly's meaning. He thought he misheard. In body, he was eminent. Standing on the roof in two-piece suit, he gazed into his distant pasture where deer were chewing the cud. The housefly flew off. It began to blow hellfire.

The housefly started large blazing fires in the Boston Common. So, the parks caught on fire, and it took all Larify's deer and horses to escort hookers from the park for they did not really notice the difference. Thousands of people in blue helmets used urns of water from the Mississippi, bolting from one center to another until *Larify.co*'s urn centers put out all flames in any of the "…worthless iron buildings among the mighty brick ones." Larify had once decreed this architectural commentary whilst drunk in public. Then the unthinkable happened again. He realized, 'I need to do something about the fly.' He thought he would seek out legal advice from those at Bladorade, a parent beverage company. Larify visited the headquarters building with his world-flag. He sensed there was some ghost haunting their building.

Funnily enough, the ghost of the Bladorade building was beside him then, already, but Larify had trouble identifying it.

Larify was carried to the airport in a bathtub.

Since his nervous breakdown, he preferred to lay in a tub for hours at a time, and he had the money for the assistants to transform his porcelain tub with spectro gadgets and then carry the tub through the stain-glassed foyer out into the Boston street.

Then his bathtub was put into a limo that drove to New York City. Larify slid the tub out of the limo at a stoplight, then got out and stood on the street in his robe. A singing leather shoe fell from the sky.

He wondered what had thrown this shoe, and then he heard,

"I threw myself."

Larify was glad to hear from this miraculous shoe. Though, he could not use it to call people. He would need his Jiv 10 for that. Larify then picked up this shoe and carried it forth and went to a rugged homeless street urchin and tried to give him the shoe, but the man said,

"Oh God. No, please."

The shoe was also refused by fans who posed to take pictures with Larify. They wore *Larify.co* t-shirts, posing outside a large black building with a mural painted on the side of it.

They shook his hand, but did not hear Larify ask, "What am I?" cause he did not ask it. Larify started walking up the street and repeated "What am I,'" "What am I," "What am I." His assistant found him and led him back to the warmed tub.

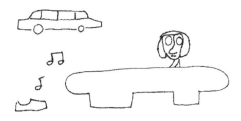

Arriving at the airport, Larify's limousine followed the course to the private runways. A large spinning digital coin rotated above his black limo. Many of the people who were in lines to fly commercial became excited. Larify wore his robe and dragged his feet up a staircase and into the small jet. Leaning into the aisle, Larify told his assistant, "Please take the long way this flight." The assistant relayed this to the pilot. The plane shot off from a private airport. It headed west, going at the proper speed to catch the proper lighting of a certain wheatfield. Larify adored this particular field of wheat. In hours, Larify got the eye feast. A mile below his seat, there were swaying, golden grains. Within a bordering forest, streams in the tributaries dallied against pebbles, and the treetops blocked the plane's shadow. Water was wearing away the pebbles below the leaves. This modest yet concentrated ministry of the water continued.

The airplane began to turn.

Sun lit the plane's undercarriage, just as it lit the golden wheat field and one grasshopper idling on a stalk. Larify fell asleep in a plush, white seat. When he woke up half-way through a nap, he noticed the housefly aside the plane.

It was flying and weighed at least ten pounds.

A couple of hours later, Larify woke up again. He forgot he was anyone. Slowly, Larify gathered the story of himself, looking quizzically at his ID card as the plane's barber cut his hair. Larify fit into a heavily starched suit de mode. It made his shoulders boxy. In a suite, he practiced public speaking with a voice recording hologram. Larify had sex thirteen times, and then he went to this meeting with Bladorade's people. On the drive there, he used his Jiv 10, a new cellphone device. Larify trusted the inventors of the time-space were doing the same as him in life, and in recent years, the tech camps had made rapid improvements. Instead of a crumpled telegram, Larify used a Jiv 10.

He would use the razzle dazzle device to call someone he thought was his friend.

Larify pushed a button.

"Hell-o."

"Hell-o."

It was Millcat, his number one business friend. Millcat had a meteor for a head and a fuzzy mouth. At least, that's how he was in person. Otherwise, Millcat was an executive with a sharp exacting glare, no time, and a bunch of priorities. The two had been working as water tycoons at the same time. Millcat was one of Larify's best Earth friends. By then, it was typical in the early 2000s to collaborate with people one didn't like. Millcat did not like Larify, but Larify did not know people would still talk to you but not tell you they do not like you.

Millcat was impatient.

"Hell-o," he said once more.

Larify's eyes adjusted.

He was in the elevator.

He was inside Bladorade headquarters.

"This is Larify."

"I know."

"Ha. I was wondering."

"You and your jokes, Larify."

"Listen, I'm a bit confused. I –"

"I'll listen to you then give up. I'm big important man. Anyway, *I* was just wondering – how much money will it take to rename the world Millcat?"

"Well, let me get a figure."

Larify asked his assistant for a number.

Millcat said to his own assistant,

"No – no get them out of here because it looks less."

"Did you say something Larify?"

"No."

"Good."

The dread Larify encountered in a bathtub weeks ago seemed to be constantly awaiting something.

Millcat and Larify seemed to understand one another for years. But now, Millcat made bigger dealings. Larify was rising in a skyscraper. The hallways were filled with bargaining yuppies looking at the margins. They squawked on many Jiv 10s. So Larify relied on a recent memory to find something familiar. He had no family per say. The brights were one with his soul. Sun had beamed through his foyer's stained-glass window the day before when his tub was carried to his limo.

"Ah," said Larify, on his Jiv. "Look – look – I was just wanting to ask you something. See, I am from an odd star system..."

"Oh no, me too," said Millcat. "Aren't these Jiv 11s fantastic?"

"They are."

"..."

"I am now going to see Bladorade's head people, you know. The ones with huge names. I'm going to get this old ally of mine out of my head. You see, when I saw the ocean I landed on a housefly and it told me there were two hard facts about life. The first fact is that your body is going to die but you must feed it. The next is that all things will leave you."

"Money, Larify."

"What do you mean?"

"Money," Millcat repeated.

"…"

"I need to know, by the way, Larify. Did your transponder light up yesterday?"

"No."

"Did your transponder notify you?"

"No."

"It didn't signal? Man. Alright, bye."

Larify exited the elevator off his Jiv 10.

He sat down in the perimeter of the business office. Bladorade had many nice countertops. Office workers sat flicking their fingertips. There were black keys with fingerprints all over the building. But the coffee was far away, and the cafeteria vending machine was out-of-service. Matter of fact, the vending machine's screen caught on fire. Larify was at a loss for words. Everywhere, things were happening like he expected, but new things in his heart needed to remain there and he could not identify them.

Larify was heavily inexperienced, unable to process his experience.

Larify waited in fire.

He recalled a recent memory again.

His tub had been hoisted down his staircase. A burst of sunshine came into the stained-glass foyer. It pierced clouds. A prodigal sunbeam is called, 'A finger of God' by the Irish. A glare had made Larify blink his eyes and then Jeford flew to his side.

Open-mouthed, the bright said,

**35**

"The next time I live, I wonder what I ought to be."

"The next time?"

"My life, yes."

Larify had nodded like a 37 year-old.

"Jeford," said Larify, in his own skin. "I am starting to feel like this place may not need me as much as I thought."

"Oh."

"Yeah, I wonder why I'm here."

"Just die then," Jeford recommended.

That was his memory.

Then Larify got another call on his Jiv. It was a telemarketer. Larify shut his eyes. When he opened them there was a blind man with silver eyes and snow-colored hair sitting at a secretary's desk. Larify exclaimed, "Moondog, it's you!" This was one of Larify's favorite composers. He had lived from 1916 – 1999, part of the time in America. They listened to the song "Friska." It was dark and ugly. It made Larify think, 'worms in the dirt – worms in the dirt – worms in the dirt.' Larify looked around his body. The waiting room where Larify was asked to "be patient" in needed a fresh coat of paint. If not, it was going to remain flaky and plaque colored. The room was also airless. It was stuffy. There was not a single window.

The chair he was put to was quite janky.

Nevertheless, Larify hummed "Friska" as he heard Moondog's song playing in the room. Larify noticed the fly land on an office chair in the corner. He felt uncomfortably astonished. Finally, a black-haired woman led Larify to the "good" elevator. The doors opened. Larify was led down the hallway to a meeting room. It was colder in the hallway then in the room, and Larify saw a window overlooking the city of Atlanta. Then Larify noticed the two CEOs of Bladorade looking at him. One of the CEOs had a diamond earing. Larify did not register this as meaning wealth, though he was distracted by the light reflecting off the man's ear that ricocheted from the window.

Larify sat at the chestnut table. At the same table, there was a lawyer and a paralegal who had stockings on her legs.

Larify said, "I want to quit."

The lawyer said,

"I will be sure to listen."

They got right to it.

"So, Larify," said one CEO. "The blood giant is putting on a choop drink. It will be a party for only the hottest US people."

"Big shots."

"We suggest you come."

"Okay," said Larify. "I would like to have a sort of... *moral* discussion. I considered something just now. My friends have been stealing things for years. I've made at least fifteen girls cry."

"I've checked your trajectory," said one CEO.

"Hmm."

"If we do not use *Larify.co* for branding early next year, you stand to make less money."

The CEOs agreed.

"I – I did something just now. I stepped on an ant on my way in. I may not want to do business. I don't think I'm fit for business. I quit. It is the millennium by the way."

One CEO activated a hidden recording device.

Larify tried to call on his lawyer, but the lawyer was asleep. His arms were folded on the table. One of Larify's assistants would have filled him in on mature business strategies, but his assistant was in the bathroom sexting. His limo driver was staring off into street space chewing some one-of-a-kind cheese baguet for $14 bucks.

"Look," said Larify, "I am glad you are trying to tell the truth here."

He regarded the window.

"The sun is out there though."

"The choop drink will be exquisite," assured a CEO.

"I don't think the actual sun gets too close to other stars, like where I'm from."

No one in the room got this. Rather, no one in that room admitted they got this, or tried. Larify started to daydream out the window. He noticed the black eyes of small birds. There were pleasantries involved. It was good to see other people, however, as the meeting continued Larify's attention was hijacked by a three headed pigeon perched level with the windowsill. The creature was holding the bones of a scientist in a cage. Alas, it was the skeleton of the naturalist Charles Darwin.

Next, there came the giant idea of Competition. Then there came Survival as a concept. At last, there came the colossal, alabaster Bureaucracy. It was a most large and imposing horde. The giants were wriggling thin fingers and worked through the yuppies who were no longer thinking of children's puppets or cartoonish emotions since they had to be millionaires. Their goals were somewhere. In the US, people forget they live in relative luxury and do not need to be afraid for their lives any longer like they had been for thousands of years living on plains. Larify signed a few documents to get himself out of the boardroom posthaste. The stress on the hearts in that business would surely wear on the hearts.

Big ideas were afoot.

Alas, few of the employees had studied.

There were only a few magnifying glasses in the drawers of desks.

The final Bladorade meeting would end up losing Larify money. He gave up on corporate. In the lobby, his assistants had his bathtub heated.

One asked,

"So, did you get real things done?"

"Perhaps," said Larify.

He jabbed down his world-flag.

Then he asked,

"Would you mind putting my tub down in that square we passed earlier?"

"Okay boss."

"Thank you."

In a nearby square, there was a statue of an eagle and a human. At the base of that statue an inscription read, 'Health Is Freedom.' People were sitting around on black iron benches saying, "Nah – Nah – Nah." Larify had asked kindly that his tub be placed down in a common so that he could soak.

He was still wearing his business suit.

Light was construing the time of 7 o'clock. It was making visceral and enchanting plays in the square. A hippie man came to Larity holding a flower with torn roots.

"We want peace, man," he said.

But Larify did not want to join any competition at first. He was frightened by what he saw happening to people in the business sector that he was not in. Moonlight soon lit the water which had to be reheated by an assistant who came and adjusted the numbers on the heater under the tub. Returning to the abiding limousine, this assistant was deathly scared that he would lose his job and stability, unsure how he had gotten himself into a place where his livelihood was determined by an odd purple man who took baths in public.

Larify foresaw this.

As the prospect of Larify's money went, so did approval of his character. Larify leaned over his bathwater and made a call on his Jiv 10 to an affiliate who remained good to him.

"You know the championship jerseys made for teams who didn't end up winning? Their championship jerseys were made, yes? Right, where are them? All the names...yes. Okay, well acquire what's left in stock. We will deliver those jerseys to homeless shelters."

"..."

"Okay."

"..."

"Yes. Happy millennium."

In the sky, there was the orange moon.

It was the lifeless skull, given cognizance by sunlight.

The sun was shining on the bottom of the globe. Larify shuddered and said, "Oh how time has passed," and smiled, somewhat diabolically. He remembered reading of American history and seeing the depression in the 20s. As a spectator, he figured a lot of the US' represented history was boring and missing slivers.

There was sheer irreverence toward Art History in many pockets!

Then he looked at his Jiv 10s Google feed and saw mania.

He called his banker on the electronic device.

"Yes, it is Larify."

Blah.

Blah.

Blah.

"Liquidate my assets."

He called his limo driver.

"Sell my limo for two hundred dollars."

Then he played Moondog's song "Frost Flower."

## 7.  Days of the Tub


Larify forgot the world. His body was lying in a formal suit. He was in a bathtub placed in a square in Atlanta. Closing his eyes, the bright shut off his sight from buildings, levels, police sirens, hard, hard hearts, pending email-responses, and he played 'What is here? What is there?' in the darkness. Boston, Bladorade, and Bureaucracy became irrelevant. Extended lines of time did too. The potential panic of his assistants did not affect Larify under water. There was no issue. There was nothing to obtain but the glory of Larify's own experience.

Easy for him to think, I think.

One day into his public tub soaking, the water became murky.

His refuse yellowed it.

By the second day, 202 photos of "The tub dweller" had been digitized and pegged. His face was always open and breathing. A police officer tried to be bothersome, but one of Larify's assistants stopped the authority from shaking him, saying, "This is part of his process." The assistant was thinking Larify might die or have his own *Eureka!* moment like Archimedes. This could fix Larify's current lack of interest in professionalism. From windows adjacent to the square, those trying to birth, liven, spin, and end the world, stared from their windows and were struck conscious by the man asleep in a tub. The apartment dwellers were seeking enlightenment. They were egged on by charlatans posting on their networks. Extraverted, short-attention spans were popping up on screens telling the 'followers' regurgitated advice. They did so before self-knowledge or regard for the current knowledge of the individual who was to read the information. These false people were a typical spectacle at the web's beginning. Larify hoped people would learn to do less on their own if they were ever going to meditate.

Inspired by the man in his white tub, who might have been dead, the observers overlooking the square from apartments stepped back. They shut their shades, and in their own ways, they forgot the world, too. There were trees in the common around the square with rounded arrays of branches and their yellow and brown leaves were dropping every hour. Birds perched in those thinning branches but also flew in flocks over the square as if practicing formations was what the birds liked. A few novice bird watchers knew it is always a hoot to try and see what birds on a powerline are jittering or puffing breasts. Cars and trucks scooted by on a street aside the square. Small trails of white smoke unfolded from tail pipes to disappear. Doctors, teachers, nurses, curators, aspiring business doers, aspiring socialites, gamers, computer science majors, all of these vocations were practiced by people walking through that square. There were at least nineteen hot bodies who felt effected by Larify's public soak in the tub. They left him alone but seeing Larify changed their day. One stranger noticed Larify and the stranger's heart began to quiet. It felt less torn than it had in a very long time. Another heart combusted. The leaves scattered. Some people seeing Larify were able to sort out how bird sounds came from beaks, whereas the dumb or brutish noises were often sounding from people whose voices sounded like a yodel. Between foreign human voices and the chirps and whistles of bird beaks, there were certain imagined sounds – like cruel things said in low tones by dear people – the sound of one's own name – pitches of black despair. These sounds spread apart like clouds in the sky. Less people were afraid. There was no hurt in the falling sunlight that did not hurt. For Larify's silence, a routine day became fresh and good to many people around him.

How could he fathom their other lives?

Others who went on to cross the streets around the common even noticed that it was the rusty trucks and sleek cars and a hatchback or two that rumbled.

It was not the sapiens sitting behind the wheels of the machines, though the operators in their cabins seemed inseparable from the vehicles most days both to themselves and others, illuminating only at night to check center consoles.

Larify had soaked for three entire days. A boy sitting aside that square on a hill thought many things. Larify's financier had relocated *Larify.co*'s exorbitant funds and donated the majority of the bright's money. Just after the black limo was sold, one of Larify's assistants was beginning to fret that he was doing his job without pay for it.

The two assistants and the limo driver came from a near coffee house to check on Larify and the tub's temperature again, and one assistant thought, 'The boss is batty for keeping his eyelids closed like this in a public area.' The limo driver said the same thing aloud, then said, "…what with what is going on in Beirut and all." The other assistant shut his eyes imitatively. However, this certain person could not go a full minute without worrying that others might hit him. Later that afternoon, there was a small bright cloud that burst and through it flew Timjiffery amidst a whole fleet of itty sparkles. Spending time with pseudo-Irish men that shrugged and woofed like oafs in parks, Larify's contemporary had gained the trust of a faerie squadron. Timjiffery was glad he was a bright and not the pesky earth spirits, the fairies, who were zipping to and fro, for they were being a nuisance, and a bright was naturally either inside their star, or else floating observantly about the universe. By nature, fairies are only seen fleetingly by the Irish with only some Irish in their blood, and the fairies would play jokes on those cutting through the square at night because it was late, and the stragglers were out at night thinking they knew too much. Above, around the Bright Common, brights were looking through ether wells. The deep circles showed the sides of other planets.

Only a few brights huddled beside one well and saw Larify lying in the water, being very still, facing the universe with closed eyes.

The faerie swarm was in the square.

The archangel Michael flew in.

He remained on high over a man with his arms crossed.

The phenomenon hovered silently with his back to the sun. A great psychoanalyst named Sigmund once called such phenomena as fairies or angles *neuropsychosis of the defense*: a hallucinatory confusion that will protect the ego from dealing with something the ego cannot face in real life, such as business failure or divorce. However, does this presuppose the brain or his thinking originates before renderings of light? It is fair to deduce these fantastic things do exist to some, and many people over the history of Earth never heard of psychology but may have seen a faerie squadron.

Or were they leprechauns? The ether is busy with so many things!

On the fifth day of Larify's public bath, people organized a rally around what they thought to be Larify's 'demonstration.' Then there came an opposite side immediately. The rabblerousers were simplistic. The butchers were haughty. A day later, Larify opened his eyes. The tub water was green with bacteria and tiny brown frogs were waiting by Larify's side, surprised themselves that he had not been a log. The square had a number of sharp street people. There were also pikes, pamphlets, and other trappings of the group that tried to attend Larify's act of 'conscience rebellion.' The bad breath of the other group lingered. Having explored darkness, Larify sat up and looked about. The Earth had rotated five full times. Larify turned, he saw the pamphlets and signs abandoned on the ground, too, but Larify felt like he was in a wholly different square. Excitement occurred. Larify laid there next to his world-flag, which had been stored underneath the bathtub.

## 8. The Hairy Creature

Larify rose from the bathtub, bashful and quiet, and he moseyed forward, planting his world-flag then walking right foot, left foot, again and again. He crossed the street to sit on a hill and rested his back against a lone tree. Since the water in the tub was mucky, Larify's waterlogged hands were a greenish hue. There were highly sensitive people in a street huddle. They stood in a nearby parking lot keeping watch. Larify saw outbursts from a distance and heard, "Sunna – we're dri – oh – aw na," until he acknowledged these people with his mind and they started to laugh, though it was unclear if they ever meant to talk at Larify in the first place. The sunset burnt off amazingly bright colors. When crossing the street, Larify heard cars driving over the roads. The increased lucidity of sounds did not register with Larify until he had been sitting there on the hill for a minute. Long flat clouds stilled in the sky. Glancing into his wallet, Larify saw plastic cards, cash, and soiled bits of paper. He remembered when he first came to Earth with no credit cards. This reminded him of his first memory – his fellow brights lording over the ether wells. The color changing common with buttressed ceilings in a star was far away. In this moment, he felt closer to the ground than he had ever been.

A darkness set over the park. Then Larify saw a figure walking across the sports fields, striding speedily. It threw up its claws and made dog noises. Squinting, Larify saw a werewolf with a round pot belly that seemingly discomforted it, for the creature kept touching its stomach as it walked upright through the baseball field, wearing a blue ballcap on its head and holding a cone of pink cotton candy.

The werewolf howled, "awooooooo," then chomped the cotton candy, and dropped a baseball bat from its knee-high khaki breeches, leaving the souvenir baseball bat in the grass by the dugout. This werewolf happened to have a pension for all things British, and it had a small Union Jack lilting from its pocket.

As the werewolf walked along the first base line toward the outfield, Larify received a call on his Jiv 10.

It was Millcat.

"Hello," said Larify.

"Larify, Hell-o."

He could not help but smile.

"Larify, not sure why you just called me."

"…"

"But I need to say that you should lose my number," said Millcat.

The werewolf, passing by, seemed to sniff something in the air. Its neck snapped and it faced Larify, then it got down on all fours and started to chase its tail, gnawing at the bushy hairs when it caught its tail.

Millcat said,

"Now, to me, you are what is called 'a liability' in the biz. Is everything alright upstairs in that odd brain? Everyone is saying you've lost it. *Everyone*. My company stands to make far more money than yours now and I need to do what is right."

*Beep – Boop – Beep*.

Larify's cheek pressed a few buttons.

"The projected growth of Larify.co has plummeted in the recent reports, too," said Millcat. "It is an absolute sinker. I can't be associated with such a failure, you understand?"

"…"

"What! No, it looks less. Keep that there."

The werewolf watched Larify with one eye, then it started to growl and chomped at the cotton candy covered in dirt. It growled and growled. Millcat continued on about something, but Larify's jiv device went *boop* again. Larify ended the call. The werewolf crept up the hill toward the bright. It growled. Larify swore he heard it say, "Thank God." Larify tried to take a picture of the werewolf, but after the flash, there was only the slope of the hill in the photo, and Larify rubbed his eyes. Having achieved initial enlightenment, Larify still considered his feeling and view to belong to his body alone, so there remained a divide between himself and the werewolf, and unbeknownst to Larify, who simply pouted his lips as the creature neared, this lack of unity angered the werewolf, and the hairy creature sneered, and Larify, in his heart, felt something was wrong.

He tensed, then scooted closer to the tree.

Suddenly, the werewolf stood upright again. It pouted and began to sniffle.

"Oh, you are cold!" wept the werewolf.

"…"

"Whyfor?" it asked.

He looked at Larify.

"Where am I?" the wolf said, looking left and right.

It was as if the creature forgot what it had been doing just a moment prior.

Larify waited for himself to speak, then said,

"This is a park, in a southern state, in a country of states, during a very special time."

"Oog."

"Do you know it is the millennium?"

"*Do you know it is the millennium?*" the werewolf mocked.

Larify squinted.

"Don't you know the British?" the werewolf quipped.

The street huddle nearby started to wiggle. Larify saw how the bathtub he abandoned had been drained and occupied by a man at rest.

**47**

"Ew," said the werewolf, leaning toward Larify, who remained sitting down against the tree. "You do not smell good."

Larify stood up to walk and talk with the werewolf, and as they moved through the eyes of the public, they jerked and jittered, and now and again, the werewolf would take out its Union Jack and spin the flag over his head. Larify walked at a steady pace with his world-flag, acknowledging strangers and passing through the electric light that fell from convenience stores into parking lots. The werewolf explained to Larify that he had been sick for three years. Whenever there was a full moon, he would grow excess hair, fangs, and he would forget where he was.

Larify looked up at the moon. It was a waning gibbous, as a matter of fact.

"I need to get back to the Dakotas," said the werewolf, as they approached a clothing store.

"Okay," said Larify.

"Will you come with me?" asked the werewolf. "If you do, I'll grant you an introduction to things you have never seen before."

"Like what?" asked Larify.

The werewolf spun around, put his claws together and showed his teeth excitedly.

"I've been bloody depressed, you see. I've been caustically low to the sun. So, others have been keeping me willing to live. They are the ones, godly ones, who have a clue, a scooby, about life. They are old and stable. They are ancient in existence."

When Larify took out his Jiv 10 again to look up something on the Internet, the wolf howled. Larify looked up.

"Pay attention!" said the werewolf.

Larify bought himself a thin autumn jacket and sweatpants and stood as a spectacle at the register. He and the werewolf used his credit card at a motel.

The motel room's bedspread had geometric puke for a pattern. The rug stayed on the floor, like the silence of the long abused. Larify sat on the bed, but the wolf, suddenly enraged, went on sieging the hotel room. It began to tear up the cheap carpet then and growled as it shuffled around the room and peeled up patches of the rug with its claws and sent frayed slices of the carpet airborne. Larify, picking out his ID from his pocket, read his name, birthdate, New Orleans and thought, "Oh yeah." He looked at the werewolf and asked, "What is your name?" Standing by the curtains and heater, the rueful werewolf stared at Larify with its black eyes. It had thin furry arms that hung aside its potbelly. The creature was embittered by incessant formality. The language of humanity was so offensive to the werewolf, for it did not replace the lack of concern for others. A man passed by the hotel room's picture window, emphasizing something with his hands. Larify remembered himself, the living, and could have given in to personal convenience. He could have returned to business with the likes of Millcat. He looked at the wall, feeling alone.

Larify did smell quite bad.

"No – I don't think I do know the British," said Larify. "I'm not here for that."

"Oh…so you're just here for yourself?"

"I don't think so," said Larify.

"Am I lost?"

"How do I know?" asked the bright.

"I don't know," said the werewolf. "I am lost, but I feel everything. And I feel the US numbness, too. Don't you?"

"Yes, sure," said Larify.

The werewolf went to the window. He took off his ballcap, cupped it to his heart and folded an arm behind his back.

"Tomorrow, you need to consult the Acorn Oracle. It has been arranged. When you wake up, just look out the window."

As he lay under the ugly blanket on scratchy sheets, Larify reflected. While he studied on the moon, Larify thought the people would all acknowledge his insight and trust it was the millennium and that no one really needed to fear lacking security as God was taking over and life could be peace, and that was just swell, but he had a nervous system now, and his teeth were chattering. In a sense, the US deserved true freedom and Larify could be an example of a free person himself. Though, he had learned something only humans know: It is far easier to speculate like a bright on feelings of a single life than it is to be a physical man waiting in a hotel in November unsure where you belong, sleeping beside a temperamental hairy creature that refuses to give its name.

## 9. <u>Acorns</u>

Jeford was soaring through air in the state of Maine. Larify's old friend floated into a moonlit tree, then looked into a house. Sitting on a couch, there was a young woman resting after a day of school. Jeford hoped the woman would still be alive when he got to live. He saw a device light up the woman's chin and sweatshirt, and he thought, 'I could be that little light.' Wind blew the array of thin branches.

Meanwhile, Larity was sitting in a hotel room with the werewolf. At the corner, across the street, Larify saw the ghost of his favorite painter – Jean-Michel Basquiat. The master painter was standing with braided hair, wearing an ethereal trench-coat. When Larify exited the motel room, the werewolf was drinking a cup of tea. Larify followed after the ghost of Jean-Michel. They walked on the sidewalk. In the US, it is unclear whether spirits or military soldiers are patrolling the neighborhoods. In recent history, the spirits here have regimented. Larify followed Basquiat to an apartment building. They walked up the staircase. On the fourth floor, Jean-Michel passed through a door. On the other side, a voice asked,

"This man's not going to bring any of that outside world in here, is he?"

Jean-Michel did not know.

When the door opened, Larify was faced with a pillow. The pillow had a neck. It was attached to a man's body that was wearing a green sweater that had a tare at the collar and tares in the front of it. The kitchen had a checkered floor and a table where Basquiat sat down with two other ghosts. It was evident the pillowheaded man had been taking tea with the ghosts of Moondog and Robert Lax, who was back visiting the country from the island of Patmos. The two tall ghosts welcomed Jean-Michel non-verbally and then looked at Larify.

"You're back," said Lax.

Following the pillowheaded man into a different room, Larify entered a den, where there was a crescent shaped loveseat by a radiator. The room was trapezoidal, and the drapes seemed to make the outside sunlight blur. Sunlight made the whole den look beige at that hour. There was a bookshelf, a glass table, and a leather couch.

The pillowheaded man sat down on the couch and pulled at his sweater.

Larify sat in the loveseat.

"I'm Larify," said the bright.

"That's great," said the man with a pillow for a head.

"…"

"I am the Acorn Oracle. My signals tell me you've chosen to see more of the country than the industrious front."

"Yes," said Larify, "I got my eyes in a space cart nearly a decade ago now."

"You know, it is good. You notice there are at least two totally different perspectives and one is clearly more important and over time it encompasses the other. Of course, the final perspective is the natural proceedings of Earth."

From his pocket, the man took out a pouch. He poured a dust of acorn bits into his palm. Two unblemished acorn caps were well preserved. Three whole, round acorns rested. Between these larger pieces, there were small bits of crushed acorns. Picking up one whole acorn, the man eyed a circular hole in its shell. Confirming something to himself, the pillowheaded man exhaled then nodded.

"Larify, is it?"

"Yes."

"Coo – coo – coo."

"…."

"Coo – coo – coo – coo."

The oracle was cooing to his acorns. Then he listened with a side of his pillow.

"You crunched 72 acorns over the past three months. 72 is less than average for your age demographic."

"How do you know how many acorns I cracked?" asked Larify.

"They tell me."

"Who?"

"The acorns. Not *who* but *what*."

"How does that work?"

"How much time have you got?" asked the man with a pillow for a head.

"I can stay till the afternoon."

The oracle began to move the acorn pieces around in his hand.

"Tonight, the werewolf and I are beginning our journey to South Dakota."

"*Eves*," said the pillowhead. "The werewolf's name is *Eves*."

"Ah."

"You have only one day?"

"Yes."

"That is not enough time to explain my acorn knowledge, sorry."

After putting acorns back into a pouch then putting the pouch into his pocket, the acorn oracle with a pillow for a head went on to give a lengthy explanation about the types, sizes, and behavior of acorns.

'I'm not sure why that is useful information,' Larify thought.

"I never said it was," said the pillowhead aloud, having sensed Larify's innermost thoughts. "Neither did oak trees. But I am a US citizen. I can think how I like."

"…"

"See there?"

The pillowheaded man pointed to his two full bookcases.

"I have 33,000 souls in my bookcase."

"Wow."

"What is fiction?"

"Well – I don't know."

"I myself was collecting watches," said Larify.

The oracle stood up and walked into a bedroom next to the kitchen. Larify could see stains on the back of the oracle's pillowcase. The oracle came back holding a contraption of twisted and bent coat hangers. He set the contraption on his floor, then fiddled with the outlying hooks and connected one hook to a well-preserved coat hanger that he used to raise the contraption slowly. Holding the transportive coat hanger with one hand, the man lifted open a window. He stuck his shoulders out, looked up, and finding the sun in the sky, he began to shout aggressively,

"By 10 AM on the fourth day my antenna here is going to steal the wi-fi signals from Mexico and Peru and Nicaragua, causing a blackout that will affect all government and digital surveillance across North America."

"..."

The oracle stepped away from his window. He rested the coat hanger antenna on the floor.

"I've been working on it for 4 years."

Larify realized this was not going to work.

"It's not going to work though," the oracle admitted.

He sat back down.

He pressed his hands together.

"..."

"So – do you know about *closed systems*?"

"I don't."

The pillowhead exhaled his disappointment.

"Look – I'll put it to you like this; you are going to live a lot longer than you expect, Larify. So you better get used to having values or things to play with in your eyes or you are going to be subject to all the flashing notes they are selling out there."

"Do you think US people are a happy people?" Larify asked.

"No," said the pillowhead. "People are awful. They only appear happy to spite me because I am infinitely important."

"Really?"

"No. Fool."

The men both considered things and looked at different spots in the den. Soon Larify realized they had not spoken for almost a half-hour. It seemed like they had been sitting together for an entire day, not just a late morning. Sunlight made the whole den look the color of honey at that hour. The pillowhead began to look at his wall clock as if he had a later appointment. There was a desk between the den and kitchen. Above the desk there was a sign. It read, "Great minds do not equate to single sentences." One of Moondog's albums was playing in a CD player in the kitchen. Time was dragging. Larify stared into the side of the pillow, where the actual pillow was bulging from the pillowcase. Every insecurity Larify had picked up on Earth came into his stomach and so did anger. He did not like the oracle's mode of explanation and wanted to leave. Nevertheless, the message was given; "You are going to live a lot longer than you expect, Larify."

Minutes later, Larify stood outside a bar with golden writing on the front of it and went inside to have an alcoholic beverage. Traditionally, when a person in the US witnesses a happening that is inconceivable or supernatural, like a meeting with ghosts or an acorn oracle, intoxicants are used because the world as they once knew it seems upside down. The bar glowed in blue neon light. Larify had five shots of whisky, got into three shoving matches, and then climbed a wall, holding onto an old wall-mounted cask and refusing to come down or give back a bottle of gin like a thieving monkey.

Larify sat down, wobbling, and kept listening to blithe Irish riddles.

"Angel's share," people said.

"I ain't brining nuddin to the cookout," people said.

"It's the millennium," Larify maffled, "...the peaceful millennium."

They did not kick Larify out for a while. Then the police came and the purple man was taken away in a paddy wagon in handcuffs. The next morning, Larify was freed from a drunk tank while still drunk. The mugshot they took made it look as if skin was falling from his face. A fraction of his skull was skinless. The mugshot was put on the Internet. On threads about Larify of *Larify.co*, people started to post things like, "Larify is inhuman and ugly!" There were seventeen videos posted on advertisement platforms. People would talk about Larify's erratic behavior for two entire weeks. While sleeping in the drunk tank, Larify had many dreams, including a glimpse of the oracle with a pillow for a head who was saying,

"Once, my mind was a candle encased in glass, but I put a pillow over it to preserve the flame. Now my head is soft. And you know what? God's honest. It is nice. I don't understand people too well, but I don't pretend I do. Out there, in the hubbub, people don't like to pretend at what they are doing so much as they could if they listened to higher organization. I understand acorns, books, and I wield a coat-hanger satellite."

## 10. The Grass-Stained Astronaut

Outside the pen, a hooptie pulled up and parked on the other side of the street. A *hooptie* is a name for a car. Larify stood outside of the police station moping. The window of the hooptie rolled down and a hooded driver said, "Come on. Let's get going." Recognizing it was Eves the werewolf, Larify walked across the street. They drove forward and Larify looked at his Jiv 10 and scrolled through a bunch of 'Larify' headlines. There were so many headlines it seemed to defeat the purpose of an objective report. Larify started to wonder if there was anything 'true' the people of the United States agreed on nationally, or if all was subject to opinion. The werewolf appeared somewhat human in the driver's seat. Thick hair covered only its arms. It held its half-bald head as it drove. At a red light, the car stopped. They proceeded onto the freeway. Cars were a bane to Eves the werewolf, so all were bad drivers in his experience. "Going to need gas soon," said the werewolf. The car whooshed down a highway. The car veered into a rest station where the werewolf growled and contorted its claws because Larify had been a spoiled city slicker and did not know how to pump gas. Inside the gas station, there was a woman wearing a dirt ridden dress.

"Can I have 5 dollars?" she asked Larify.

For a moment, he thought to obliterate all currency with his world-flag, which he had pressed down to the ground at his left. On second thought, he could not deny that currency was important to people.

"I only have my credit card," said Larify.

"Okay then," said the lady. "God bless ya now and then later. Will you buy me candy, too? A pack of cigs?"

Of course, Larify would.

The woman ordered an elaborate whip cream latte as well. After paying and beginning to pump the gas, Larify asked Eves,

"Where does all this gasoline come from?"

"Pumps in the ground," said the werewolf. "Otherwise, macroeconomics, but I'm not getting into all that noise tonight."

'Golly,' thought Larify.

"I must tell you," said Eves. "I can tell the future, too."

"Oh?"

"Yes," said the werewolf. "That is partly why I get so sick at night."

Maybe Larify should have aimed to be eyelashes or something less complex like the eyelashes, the itty reminders of plenty that fall around the lives of people, greeting faces without threat in the mirror, falling into the carpet as people stand around at home. Being a person can be a doozy. The werewolf had switched into the passenger seat.

"You drive."

Larify got into the driver's seat.

"So how do we get there?"

"First we are going to New Orleans."

"Okay."

"Aren't you from New Orleans?"

"Well, I come from a star. So, I don't know how to get to New Orleans."

"Blimey. I'll tell you which route."

"Okay."

The car pulled away from the gas pump. Larify was intuitive, but he was only slightly more so than anyone else who had never driven a car. At a red light, Larify started to piece together the rules of the road, and in transit he kept waiting behind another driver when he was unsure how to move. There were clearly many orange stars in the sky. Larify thought about the brights, and how he was alive. He may be bad at it. He reckoned he ought to be thankful. For a moment he was thankful for a boil that was forming on his forearm. Larify and the werewolf smiled to themselves over the lights in the sky. But then the werewolf howled and gritted its canine teeth.

A dreadful, undefined feeling returned to the creature, and it brought up its knees and howled for the moon.

"This is not my home," it said. "Where am I?"

Since all things die, so could this incessant longing of Eves the werewolf, but even a werewolf must learn over time. Larify playfully asked for directions and continued pretending he knew how to drive a car. Luckily, it was manual. Larify looked for a diner to eat at because he was hungry. It could come out of anywhere, though, this place to eat, and the sun was rising, so Larify hunched over the steering wheel and looked up at the light in the sky.

The humming and gust of cars around the aquamarine hooptie sounded regularly.

A diner was illuminant on the roadside like a tooth.

"I want to wait in the car," Eves grumbled.

Larify walked alone into the furnished railroad cart made into a diner. He mentioned a "Happy millennium" to a row of people sitting on stools, sidestepping to an open stool himself. When he sat down, the waitress recognized who he was. On the Internet, Larify was the man who had public misdeeds, who lost his material fortune. She handed him a menu, smirked, then went away as the regulars drawled. Larify ordered macaroni because Eves had said 'macroeconomics' hours earlier.

Sitting in a diner booth nearby, there was a grass-stained astronaut. If he were not a true, practicing astronaut, he at least had an authentic astronaut suit on that made him look hyperbolically large. The astronaut spoke to his company awkwardly, not only because he was a brainy astronaut, but because he was afraid of what he might unveil with his intergalactic views. The astronaut suit was complete with a fully orbicular space helmet. Although the visor was down, the astronaut tipped orange juice from a plastic cup through the visor into his mouth. The suit had certainly been worn through a mission, for it was tanned with dirt and stained by grass. A woman was sitting next to the astronaut and two other youths faced him.

If the astronaut was saying anything, it was inaudible to Larify, who camped nearby on his stool.

"The side of the road, in Kentucky," someone in the diner said.

Many in the diner's close quarters, sitting on the red-leather upholstery, were 'in their heads,' as if neither an astronaut, nor the food was spectacular.

The astronaut was thinking. His thoughts were unfortunate.

'I rue her. I rue the other men. I rue my jealousy that I do not know. I rue fast-paced messaging. I rue the buffoonery spoon-fed to idiots. I rue how that stranger over there is probably God but I have no means of introduction. I rue how my mission was solitary. I rue how I now have the forbidden knowledge. I rue that I rue though I know astrophysics. I rue that I don't know I rue. I can't say it, so I sit and brood.'

Beside the astronaut, there was an open window. A tube went from the astronaut's pack through the window and connected to a floating parcel. The parcel was white like a clean onion and made of space fabric. Inside of it there was sunlight the astronaut had gathered. It was secret sunlight. No one was supposed to even be seeing the parcel floating from his pack, but in reality it was not very discreet.

In a few minutes, the grass-stained astronaut stood up to leave. As he waddled down the aisle, the coiled tube passed through the diner's wall as if immaterial. The astronaut exited the diner and was united with his precious parcel, crying underneath his helmet as he stood on the gravel holding *his* sunlight.

Larify soon went outside himself. Looking up, he saw the morning's moon was a waning crescent. Below Larify's sneakers, the small rocks scuffled and scraped as he neared the aquamarine hooptie. Larify opened the driver's door. Eves the werewolf was leaning against the passenger door, wearing an aboriginal helmet made of reeds.

"Where did you get that?" asked Larify.

"Shh – quiet."

A police officer walked up to the car. Eves rolled down his window. The officer bent down and asked,

"You don't love God too much, do you?"

"Course not," said Eves.

Eves was crossing his fuzzy fingers.

Larify sat stunned as the officer said, "okay" and walked away.

"Know how I told you I can tell the future?" asked the werewolf.

"Yeah."

"Okay – see that astronaut."

"Yeah, I see him."

"Let him come with us when he asks. He hates his own space in humanity. There's some promise for reform in someone like that."

The astronaut came to the window.

"Look, I know this is strange. But I've just been through something on my own. I really need a ride to New Orleans."

"We know," said Larify. "Get in."

For whatever reason, Larify saying "We know" seemed to frighten the astronaut, though the astronaut sat in the backseat.

"What's in your parcel?" asked Eves.

"Parcel?"

"Yeah, the one lofting out the window."

"I don't know what you're talking about," said the astronaut.

The three outcasts drove on estranged. Larify began to feel skeptical of the company. He had no other friends though, he told himself. He was on the ground now. He could not go on soaring around like a beam of light. He had become a man, driving a car, responsibly. They played the license plate game. Four cars in one moment had Hawaii license plates.

One license plate said '5low.' The werewolf thought it meant 'slow' while the astronaut thought it meant 'flow.'

Larify played "Elf Dance."

The astronaut liked this song, but since they were going to New Orleans, he suggested they listen to musicians from the region. He suggested "Exhibit A" by Elpadaro "Jay" F. Electronica, or mixtapes by Dwayne "Lil Wayne" Carter. At the next rest stop, Larify parked the car in a faintly lit area. A scummy man meandering around the gas pumps asked if he could ride with them, so that man and his white cat hopped into the backseat. The astronaut introduced himself in more or less the same fashion, as if there was not a parcel of secret sunlight lofting from his pack. After some time, the astronaut said,

"So, what makes you dudes different than the rest of us passing about in these automobiles?"

"Well – I'm a werewolf."

"Okay."

"And I can tell the future."

"You're not though," said the astronaut.

"Not a werewolf?"

"No. You're not, you're just not."

"How!?"

"I can't explain it in here. There are boundaries, realms and things. To some you're just dark squiggles serving some higher function of organization. I can't explain now. It makes me nervous. I just got back from being in outer space."

"Pff."

Larify did not notice he was driving incredibly slow.

"I have found that my curiosity, turned into materialism," said the astronaut, "then pessimism, hedonism, and finally, nihilism."

Larify genuinely wondered about the good of these 'isms.'

"God damnit space freak!" said the werewolf. "You're distracting the driver. Larify, put your foot down. You're going to get us caught, driving like that! The speed limit is 65 or 80."

There was a fly on the dashboard of the car.

Larify frowned.

Was it the housefly of yore?

They arrived in New Orleans. The city is still known as Crescent City to some since it was originally built on a bend of the Mississippi River. Eves directed Larify through the French Quarter. Larify parked the car outside of a blue house of the baroque style. Larify stepped out of the car and Eves and the astronaut did too. When the hobo with a white cat stepped out of the car, the stranger turned to the others and said, "I am Jesus Christ," then he did a cartwheel.

## 11. <u>God in the US</u>

Larify took his world-flag from the trunk of the car then closed the trunk of the vehicle. Seeing this, the grass-stained astronaut looked at him silly in his big hyperbolic white suit. Then, wanting defense for himself, the astronaut used a glass cutter to remove a windshield. Larify resisted the urge to bat him over the head once with the world-flag. Larify, Eves, and the astronaut walked up to the blue house. On the porch, they saw a man in a rocking chair with a blanket over his lap, teetering back and forth on the porch planks. Eves signaled to leave this man alone. The group stepped over the threshold and went into the house.

There was a staircase.

Amber lights dotted a chandelier.

"Hum."

To their left was a black frame. Inside the frame, there was a charcoal drawing by Joyce Treiman called, "Any God Will Do." Before they could draw a conclusion about the shapes, the glass liquefied. The astronaut peered into the frame.

He exclaimed, "Cripes!"

Replacing the charcoal drawing was a shadowy head.

The astronaut twitched.

Then the being in the frame said, "No, I am not who you think I am, man." The frame expanded. Fog rolled from inside the wall. A spot in the fog cleared. There appeared a gloomy shadow. This thing stood like a gatekeeper and wore a pleated robe. The 'horns' had been its ears. Its ears had terrified the astronaut. The astronaut stole away, bunching his knees up, assuming the fetal position aside the banister. "It's happening again!" he cried. The frame had spread up and down to become a rectangular doorway. Following Eves, Larify walked forward, and then he began a descent into an underground passageway.

The deity turned blue.

Suddenly, he was holding a torch. Larify noticed the rest of the light in the descending steps was celestial and they walked the length of the stairs till they got to the basement. There glowed a long, white table.

Action figures were set on thin curving shelves. There were shabtis. The figurines looked down into the room as Larify and Eves took seats. There were posters of Hollywood stars scattered on the bumpy stone. Though, vagabonds were the stars in this domain, so the faces in posters had missing teeth and matted hair. The room was illumined in spots by electronic candles that started to light. The wet fog remained within that small space, too. Two chairs were reserved for Larify and Eves. They sat facing the glowing white table.

The deity sat.

"Eves, bring me his heart."

So Eves the werewolf took Larify's heart.

How so?

He reached his furry arm right through Larify's chest then went plodding across the floor to put his own heart and Larify's into the being's claw. The hearts were weighed separately against an ostrich feather on a libra scale.

"Pass," said the thing, then it breathed in its snout and cackled,

"Larify…"

Behind the table, other blue lights were taking shape, appearing vague in the fog.

"Do you know who I am?" asked the shadow.

Larify could feel Eve's hot breath on his cheek.

The werewolf sat at his side, knowing the forthcoming might.

"I am Anubis."

"…"

"…"

"…"

"…"

"…"
"…"

"Understand," said Anubis, "this planet, birthed below the sun's grace, has had much, much, much action. You must understand, Larify, billions and trillions may at times have invented and found things like me so they could function and live with order. The societies crumble. The minds get sick. The goals lack precision. But you have been living a human life for something more…You have made the right decision to value all people and not just people like you."

"And you don't play sports," said Eves.
"…"

"Which helps," said Eves, "since you are alien and all."

"But this is a moment of atonement. If you are daft enough to think you are the owner of nature, you are going to fall short of your goal. The result will be an inaccurate life."

Anubis continued to assess Larify's business venture.

"If you want to take water from such a body as Mississippi when the US is becoming a more conscious part of the whole world and bottle it, you need to involve God."

"We require 100% of Larify.co," said Anubis.

More fog cleared.

Jackal-headed Anubis was sitting at a tabletop that was larger than it seemed to be when Eves and Larify sat facing the table. Lights began to appear to the right and left. Sitting to Anubis' left side, there was a foul, decaying object wrapped in a crusty gauze. In fact, it was a mummy! After letting the fog clear, the mummy counted its teeth with its reinserted tongue.

"I am Akhenaten with the elongated face…who changed the Egyptian facades…forever…."

Within, it groaned,

"New Kingdom."

It took the mummy two minutes to drawl out this statement. In the meantime, Larify recalled from his studies that Anubis was a being imagined long ago by people who stood on banks of the Tigris and the Euphrates.

'I know he's down there, I can't move, what do I do, I can't move.'

Anubis heard the astronaut's thoughts who was sitting in a non-pose by the door.

The man's ribs were forgotten, too.

"That one is stubborn," said Anubis.

Since Larify's heart was decent, Anubis went on as he intended.

"You are the one who transferred Mississippi water in vats, yes? We did a similar feat. We shaped jars of clay, filled them with water from the Nile and now the jars are alive years later, going 'I'm real.'"

"I'm real," said Akhenaten. "In Egypt…I had the elongated face…I changed the facades forever…I began new dominion…don't believe me…that's fine…that's been fine."

Larify did not mind being patient and listening to the mummy.

"That's good," Larify said.

"Well, bright," said Anubis. "You are from a faraway star, I know."

"Yes."

"Yes, and you are using water?"

"Ah, this is the one who wants to affect waters? Tell him we see him..." said Akhenaton, taking at least one minute to say so counting lower teeth with the reinserted tongue.

Larify saw there was a blessed chinaman at the glowing table.

"Who is that?"

"Who?"

Larify pointed to Anubis' other side.

"Ah," said Anubis. "Don't mind him so much. That is no one. Don't worry."

"No," said Akhenaton. "Worry is absolutely forbidden."

"On all accounts, shui."

Next to the Chinese, there was a bodhisattva with a rosy aura.

Then another eastern man with a red, hearty mirth at the table appeared sitting with clenched fists. Larify heard he was called, 'Bodhidharma.' In mind, Larify rode a short vision to the Shaolin Temple which is near Dongfeng subdistrict in Henan. It is said Bodhidharma meditated for nine years in a cave in the Shaolin mountains, facing a damp wall. When his eyelids enticed him to fall asleep, he peeled his eyelids off and threw them to the mountain slope where they turned into tea plants, resulting in the origin of the mountain's tea. Bodhidharma, the enlightened ruffian, sat with his feet flat on the ground.

There at the table was also Jesus, whose face was solemn. Larify realized then the unknown ghost he had sensed by his side, why, it was Jesus from Nazareth. He noticed the ghost first when he started to do business with Bladorade, though not being from the area, he did not recognize the spirit of the age-old tale. Jesus sat with a gold-wire crown.

Larify smiled.

"The millennium," he whispered, thinking of his own age-old message.

"The Mississippi is indeed a mighty river," said Anubis.

"It is."

"But Larify –"

Anubis snickered.

Then Eves the werewolf said, "You forget about the bloody fog mate."

"And so much more, Larify, and so much more. But you are a man are you not?"

"You can only handle so much."

"An umbrella or two," assured Eves.

After building *Larify.co*, Larify could remember thinking of many distractions besides being a man. He spotted the shadow of liberty peering out of a chalice that was put before Jesus Christ. "Remember why *you* chose to live," she had told him.

Larify nodded.

"What we are asking is, although you came to Earth, brought your message, have you ever considered if your enterprise is blessed by the people and animals that were already here?"

"Blessed?"

"What I mean is, is it good for the planet?"

He motioned to the beings at the table.

"If it were good for our planet, we would know. What did you think, Larify, you are a god? You have acted too rashly so far to even be a saint."

"So far..." seconded Akhenaten. "Mmm – mmm – mmm – mmm."

The jackal-headed Anubis pointed to Jesus of Nazareth, who was looking great and totally receptive after over 2,000 years.

"This man prayed toward the sun until he had a world in his eye, and no one remembered the shadow of the cross except for some mice that day who were idling around skull hill."

"Mice?"

"Yes. I forget you are now of the clay disposition and underestimate the animals. Back to why we have brought you. Heed the words," said Anubis. "There are things for God to do and you cannot expect to be doing them all. There are birds and willows and trees and afternoons – all the same – in cities, in cafes, in the electricity and pond water. There are things for you...grand, fantastic adventures. There is no need to be so materially ambitious. That is not your job."

"Dust to dust," said Eves.

"You did not birth Earth, Larify. Nor did you string all the days of time, and if you want to live accurately, you must pay your dues to what came first. None of us are you. Nor you either!" Anubis barked up at the eavesdropping grass-strained astronaut. "If we had not given you time, you would freak out yourself and evaporate that delicate purple costume into the helium sun. Some do that. Just know we are here and have been here. God. It may not help you, but it does help others, and has helped many more earthlings than your new reckoning."

"You can take your life back eventually, but do penance," said the bodhisattva. "Retire for some years. Give us time, for we have given things a process. For example," said Anubis. "If the ocean had not subsided, you would have come on your task as a spineless jellyfish trying to wiggle to other jellyfish how they will be okay. The least you can do is admit things have been in process longer than you and your thirsts."

"We have been at work," assured Bodhidharma.

## 12. The Merger


Jesus Christ remained silent and solemn, pointing through the wall to where the sun would rise the next day in New Orleans.

Larify looked at the mummy, who was the least intimidating at the table.

"Poo," said Akhenaten. "Don't look…like that…I am a pharaoh…there are many…many…many…kings…in Egypt…in history… I'll have you know, I had changed the facades of Egypt forever….the most creative pharaoh…of the New Kingdom…even my son Tut…"

Akhenaton drawled on, taking minutes to drag his tongue over the backs of his teeth. Upstairs, the astronaut had stood up, clutching his parcel of secret sunshine so close to the suit as he leaned against the entrance to the passageway. The astronaut dreamed all these things his family and church had told him long before he began going on space missions. He still thought the jackal-headed Anubis' ears were horns. To make matters worse, the astronaut had pulled out his flask and was drinking strong liquor that brought him back to painful memories in his childhood lifetime. One could imagine how determined the astronaut became after listening to whatever he thought was in his head talking downstairs. The grass-stained astronaut was on his continuous mission to get his bundle of sunshine to where it might be useful to the highest number of people on Earth, and surely, he was sick of moving in fear, and finally the astronaut could face the main opponent. First, he was afraid to confront the evil. Now, he wanted to eradicate the being. Charging down the staircase, the grass-stained astronaut pursued the opponent with an awkward shuffle, stumbling on the last step that was wooden to him, and his gloved hand grabbed Larify's world-flag.

He then lunged toward the table and threw the world-flag as a spear.

The top of the world-flag went right through Anubis' solar-plexus.

It obliterated an action figure on a shelf behind the table.

Instantly, the action figure was no longer available in any stores, not even to adamant, searching collectors who had been looking for it all over the US until their memory of that collectible erased.

The astronaut fell to the ground and gave hysterics.

Anubis put his hand on the table, rose up, went nearer to the man.

"Go inside your heart," Anubis commanded.

"But it's you. It's…"

"Go – inside."

"I don't want to go inside, I don't want to go inside," whimpered the astronaut.

From the fog, they all heard a voice, which said only "Hello," but then *oh!* Larify himself felt that dread again, like things are unconditionally as they are, and that he had been an ignoramus for wanting to live and exist, for it could feel so much worse than he ever expected it to. Things were far larger than him as a brand, and Larify cried out,

"I want my bathtub!"

Larify's outcry caused something to stir in the darkness opposite the two chairs.

The bodhisattva that sat at the table had not moved nor betrayed an emotion or judgment, sitting full-lotus.

"Timjiffery?" Larify asked, rhetorically, as if his friend from the Bright Common were in the same room.

Anubis leered at the astronaut, threatening him.

"Keep your head down!"

"Mortal rebel," said Anubis, "I have already eradicated my body from this place."

The astronaut perked up.

"So, why do you plague me?" he said through his radio.

"I am here, am I not? I believe what you seek at the risk of your health and safety is a Lucian idea apart from the physical plane, and it is a metaphor for putting this fallen world above what matters to your spirit's commune with God. It could be money. It could be fame. It could be that amber liquor right there in your flask. It could be the pride for your parcel."

The astronaut was shivering.

"Yes, this one has been stonehearted," said Anubis.

The mummy's gauze balm smelled like dirt, Larify noticed.

"You are lucky we gods are gods, and have learned to forgive, better understanding human weakness. It is thanks to this personage with the wire crown."

Jesus continued to point.

The astronaut bowed before Anubis.

"Verdaat."

Anubis pronounced some ghastly incantation in praise of Time, and as he spoke in a raspy ancient tongue, the action figures in total were rattling and rattling, and Anubis' voice boomed and stringed out the window and around the perimeter of the French Quarter. The sound stringed around the black lampposts. It imbedded itself in the steel on houses. Larify was sparked with genius from realization of the size of the sun. A hair doll in the bayou had mud knocked off its face, a poet saw the screen of a vending machine blur and contort, and a miscreant, hopeless youth in a grass mall found the perfect word for his raggedy older lover.

In the tremoring sound, while fog subsided, one of the rattling action figures fell. The turquoise shabtis rattled and rattled and rattled, and rattling and rattling, Jesus came over, picked the fallen figure up, and placed it, spinestraight, next to the other benign background idols.

The room became quiet.

The bodhisattva smiled at Larify and pointed down at its knees in full-lotus pose.

Larify noticed the bodhisattva was the only deity sitting like that.

Akhenaton began to speak again. It took him very long, and while he drawled on, Anubis got up, took a chalice filled with *Larify.co* water and Jesus put his hand on it. Then Anubis went to the astronaut and spilled water over the astronaut's orbicular helmet. Anubis barked something at Eves, who went to the table and wrote on a paper:

# Discomfort $\neq$ Toxin

The longhaired Christ looked at the message then nodded at the letter $x$.

Anubis said,

"Separate the two."

"One dart, two dart," said the bodhisattva.

"Discomfort…Toxin…tooth, tooth, tooth, tooth."

"Do not drink for the pain, or for the innocent goofs. Take each sip in your right mind, and if whisky dims your dreams, stop."

Next, Eves made up a contract for Larify. The werewolf wrote down, 'Larify agrees it makes sense to admit he is not as influential as Jesus Christ of Nazareth and then acknowledges the natural processes of Earth.' He also wrote down '…Larify.co has been divinely inspired.' Larify signed his name to the paper with these terms. He asked for confirmation that it was the peaceful millennium and the members of the table nodded and sent him away. The spirit of the accountants, which was struggling very hard to exist, bored with its eternal vocation of forgetting new minutes yet tracking every single currency across time and space, explained to Larify how *Larify.co* and the divine would merge. The business was done. The deities, devas, and Jesus himself began to dance.

Some devas put on masks and acted mischievously.

Larify had relinquished his short-term plan and felt more like one body prospering under the sun.

The dancing continued.

Larify learned very much by watching the dancing of the shadows in the dominion below the blue baroque house. There appeared a banquet of turkey and Larify and Eves ate while the astronaut was not in the mood although his spherical black visor looking into the cornucopia reflected all of the fruit he had not learned to swallow without deep trauma. Far away in a distant star, in their Bright Common, brights were looking down into the *ether wells* and a few noticed this rendezvous as something dazzling. The paranormal had been quite a rocking encounter for Larify.

The hobo they had picked up at the gas station came into the cellar from upstairs, walked over to Jesus, touched the Christ's robe and evaporated.

As the masquerade wound down, the lesser deities vanished, and Akhenaton fell asleep. It was then time for the meeting's end.

Jesus of Nazareth carried on to his next appointment.

Anubis put a claw on Larify's left shoulder, holding out his free hand in the direction of the Christ. Before walking up the stairs gingerly, Jesus said nothing new, as he had said all he needed to in his day, but he cited scripture.

He turned toward Larify and mouthed,

"A wicked and adulterous generation seeks after a sign, and no sign shall be given to it except the sign of the prophet Jonah."

He left them and departed.

"Obviously these meetings are rather involved and can be personal," said Anubis, as he led Larify back upstairs. "Take time to be a man. All the people in the world already know some things. Trust these things to know it is the millennium."

"Yes sir."

"Eves – The Nation of Islam is having a meeting in that room at midnight. I will be going. Larify, stay wise like black coal. Remember how this meeting really did occur and sleep in this house tonight. Good luck in South Dakota."

"Thank you, master," said Eves, drooling.

"Larify we will be collecting all your water."

Larify, Eves, and the astronaut slept in different rooms in the blue baroque house. When Larify woke up, he saw it was a beautiful Fall day through the window. The grass-stained astronaut was not in a bedroom, nor on any musty couch, near any dresser, or slumped on the floor. The astronaut had fled to continue his solo mission.

Walking off the porch, Larify said,

"I'm glad I'm a man."

The deities in that meeting had taken the whole of *Larify.co* by contract. Larify was unbothered. It was for the best. Though, when he and Eves looked from the sidewalk, they found the car they drove to the meeting had been stolen. The air was quite humid. A bulbous tree on the roadside looked like sorbet.

## 13. A Source

Larify had been a light for eons but a human being for less than a decade. What happened in the meeting in New Orleans wholly changed his approach. People in the US already had ancient, celestial wisdom. What varied is how much faith an individual put into their relationship with the divine. Larify realized he could live as a source of confirmation. He decided to become a pious Christian. New Orleans, a swamp of gastronomy, colorful houses, voodoo magic, and bluesy music would be where Larify paused. Larify would need a break. Just because gods are real that does not necessarily mean anything else about the world. It would take him all winter to base himself in faith. Besides, it was going to become too cold and icy if he drove on certain routes to South Dakota.

Larify got an honest job working in a storage facility. There, he met calm hardmen who pushed stock around a warehouse with forklifts. His coworkers could be heard grunting or telling about their own adventures routinely, and it was clear how even the simplest of people have their own divine encounters. Larify felt two things during this stage. For one, his body was quite tired due to the turbulent adventure he had been on for years, and second, Larify's eyes felt unfocused and imaginative on sunny days.

As he looked around the French Quarter, it was clear the Holy Spirit was leading many people around the city, and at the corners the public would see the same ghost, making it brighter with confirmation.

As he walked alone, Larify overheard people whispering,

"It is the millennium."

Larify read later in life this phenomenon of same meaning was called 'logos.'

Larify rented the first floor of a pink baroque house for Eves and himself.

The large windows were yellowed, and he left them unwashed.

The household was furnished with a frumpy couch and a queen-sized bed.

The kitchen tiles were ceramic and there was a gas stove.

In the living room area, there was a large TV. Soon Larify and Eves watched movies like *The Virgin Suicides* and *2001: A Space Odyssey*. Larify practiced being captious toward the physical plane, training himself to see the differences between movies and nature. Eves began to complain, saying, "I must get home. I must get to the Dakotas pronto," but within a month, after many visits from Jesus of Nazareth, Eves ceased speaking English. Instead of two legs, Eves started to walk primarily on his four legs. By the end of January, the werewolf had become a full-fledged wolf. Eves was content to remain indoors, trotting on and off his beanbag while he shared the fallen cheese and peperoni slices that fell off pizzas ordered by Larify.

Larify spent many nights laying in a bathtub and thinking,

"Wow, I am alive."

The state of Louisiana was funky, and he only saw his small part of it. He noticed the biases people had toward one another, and many seemed to need gestures, ways of walking, or buzzwords to conclude they were seeing the same spirit. Larify went out to work, walking very slowly and mindfully on his way home. He let himself sleep a lot. He got good rest. Seeing the zenith of the physical world was based on sense, Larify turned further within himself, realizing it was more refreshing to seek his own heart. It was then that he assumed the form of The Other. One of his eyeballs fell out. A fungus grew under his toenails. Every day, when he woke up, the world appeared to him dark, bright, and anew.

Larify liked to sit on a chair the prior renters had left on the porch. On free mornings at about 10AM, Jeford and Timjiffery descended to him from their lofty flights like milky blurs, but Larify, with a pleased smirk, assumed it was only the sunbeams. He had forgotten that lateral star he was from and the mission he had with his friends because he was on Earth.

Other brights began to haunt his house, too, but Larify was quiet-minded.

For all the large-scale issues of idiocy, miscommunication, and unhappiness, Larify found the US could be a place where he could have some land and sit and watch the land, finding his manhood in his ability to side with no one on anything, being uncompromising in his own bias of non-bias.

In five months, he felt he lived many years.

One April day, Bureaucracy came to the house. The alabaster creature hung its red head down over the bathroom window, and with a facetious grin it said,

"Larify, don't you want to drop this act?"

Larify said nothing.

Larify had started to feel that words for things like 'red,' 'couch,' or 'Larify,' were random or funny-sounding. Larify looked out his bathroom window. In his view, Bureaucracy was dying. The creature was not giving up though. It stayed near the house calling 'Larify,' 'Larify,' to remind the bright he was a man with responsibilities to society. Larify got off the toilet, wiped and walked into the living room.

"You must make your money, Larify. You have a reputation and a file that is on a server that will pervade all of space and time."

Larify saw that Bureaucracy was rather delusional. So he decided to show it away. He told the large alabaster creature to return that night. After dining with Eves, Larify went out the door with his world-flag and turned in front of Bureaucracy.

He walked to a car rental depot, paid for a black car.

Bureaucracy followed behind him officially. Larify drove all the way to Texas, for there are no beaches in New Orleans.

On the way to the beach, Larify had a telepathic battle with Bureaucracy, and while it thought,

'I'm going to get you.'

'You cannot escape me.'

Larify thought,

'You ought to educate US people about the world's history rather than tax all ventures. The US ought to have free healthcare. The human capitol ought to be self-knowledge.'

When Larify got out of the car and was walking to the beach, the moonlight made the wide sand white and crystalline.

"I have an idea of what to sell next," said Larify.

"That's a good-sounding idea," said Bureaucracy. "What is it?"

"This," Larify looked at the ocean.

"Permits will be needed," Bureaucracy surmised, "but because it will make money, we can weasel around the obstacles."

A weasel on the beach scurried by, unoffended.

"What did you say?" Larify provoked. "Say that louder."

"I said the ocean is big! We can sell it!"

All of a sudden, a wave rose and swept the creature into the water. It hollered as the tide receded and it was pulled out to the deep. At sunrise, Bureaucracy returned, though it was cleaned. It was laid down in a humungous porcelain bathtub composed of ruins from a long-forgotten civilization. It agreed to rest. Larify had sat on the beach through the night looking at the stars. A face in the sky opened. It began to sing. Then a shadow came from the rampart, onto the sand, and stood up. It was the shadow that fell from the back of The Statue of Liberty.

She scolded Larify, like a girl he dated for a short period in Boston, whose name was Magnifique one night and then woke up different.

"What are you doing on the beach all night?" said the shadow. "You need to get yourself help, Larify. You are becoming extremely abnormal. They are saying you are crazy. They are saying you are broke and poor, living in squalor."

Larify drove to New Orleans, returned inside and locked the door. The more Larify dug within himself, the more he realized he was a bright, though he was living as a man and so he would die. Brights had begun to sprinkle dust on Larify to remind him it was only an illusion when he started to wallow in the fact that he had nothing. They liked his solemn effort to be like them. Though the brights forgot, as he forgot, they were one another. For the six months Larify had rented the house, he had probably lived a few hundred years. Finally, he bought a car, and he consented to take Eves the length of his journey. Eves too had become more in touch with his condition. He had stopped asking Larify, "Where am I?" They passed Texas. Bureaucracy was left on the sunny shore as it drank ocean water from a humungous, transparent plastic cup.

"People don't understand," it mused. "I only want to do good. In any workplace, there are those who take advantage. I suppose I must work harder to assure the dialogue between people and procedure is clearer and must slow the hoarders of natural resources."

## 14. <u>Bird Dogs</u>

On their way north, a police officer pulled the car over and Larify handed the officer a quarter along with his ID and said, "Take this to Washington." Since one of Larify's eyeballs fell out he was wearing an eyepatch. He was unshaven and nearly the color maroon. The officer tried not to judge this man who had said a weird joke. Larify drove off. Stopping at gas stations, Larify collected a smorgasbord of personal attacks. He was so poor to look at it reminded others to look at themselves. Larify was a terrible man. He was ugly. He was a failure. He was a stupid man. He was captious. He was hopeless. Women thought him blind and helpless. "At least you know it now," he heard a lake say as they neared the middle of the country. He prayed for the safety of that officer, and for all officers, and for street people, and for boring people, and he believed he could really do little for others but antagonize them to stop looking to his face as something meaning anything. Larify became anti-matter. He became incredibly happy to be discontent with the physical world, though he drove cautiously and patiently. In a grocery store, he marched around, wielding his world-flag, scaring the picky people and entertaining the clerks as they put popcorn or juices on the shelves. The cabin of his car sailed north, up the North American continent, into what was once the Lakota region. The land had been one with the Lakota people. Then in 1877 it was made a piece of US Bureaucracy. Larify had no mind. Rolling plains surrounded the car. In the great open sky, there was a clear blue color hanging over the plains and pushing the earth into a sphere. Then a discoloration was noticed in the ether. A cloud of smoke spread and remained as one big electrical cloud while the smoke was wafting in all directions.

Larify saw gnashing mouths fly out of this smoke screen. Drooling fangs were what Larify noticed first about the bird dogs. They were steely blue. There must have been 200 of these hounds, ultimately, flying above the windshield.

Putting two hands on the steering wheel, Larify slowed down, as he was expert at doing now. From their clutches, some bird dogs let out eagles. The eagles had a symbiotic relationship with the flying hounds. One of the eagles came with a message to Larify's window.

"Lulu, piquant, mustard seed –," the eagle said.
"You must give us your friend there,
The wolf.
He is of us."

Eves was nestled in the passenger seat. Larify was wont to protect his friend while he was asleep. Larify trusted most things, but going with these flying animals was Eves' choice to make.

Larify told the eagle,
"I cannot give him to you right now. He is resting."

As the eagle went back to the swarm of bird dogs, the bird dogs with leathery blue wings were barking like claps of thunder in the smokey vortex. Larify pushed Eves. He was slightly afraid. Quickly, he glanced back to the road. He had not been driving cars long. He wanted to look natural to the motorists, though only one car every so often had driven by southward. The wolf blinked, and it saw all the bird dogs in the sky with curious notice.

There came a second messenger eagle.

It said,
"This wolf is of us. He has even parented bird dog pups."

Larify noticed several young dogs with black wings flying around. These looked far cuter and more enticing.

Five bird dogs were keeping low to the ground and frolicking with one another as there were no longer neighboring cars on the skinny road through the plains.

Then the bird dogs froze. They hooted like apes.

Out of the electrical cloud, there pounced a sabretooth tiger. It roared loudly. To Larify's surprise, Eves leapt out through the car window. Eves radiated a rosy hue and grew heavy as he grrrred.

The battle between Eves and the mustard-yellow sabretooth tiger lasted seven minutes and Larify was too surprised to make sense of the animal fighting. Both animals got in lashes and swipes. Finally, Eves lay on the ground, fatigued. The sabretooth turned to bone and sank into the sand. However, Eves rose up and grew wings like a bird dog. Larify squinted his eyes. A third eagle came to the car window.

"Huzzah," it said. "One thing you did not know about Eves was he is actually a dire wolf. A grand one who was on a pilgrimage."

Eves had slayed the sabretooth, earning a proper welcome back from the bird dogs which barked like fireworks. Then Eves went away. You see bird dogs, like Larify, have certain values and objectives they live by; this species winds in and out of temporal nature. Their barks can be loud and scary, but they want peace. They use noise because they do not mean to cause physical pain to humans. Larify contemplated. He was now abandoned on a road trip. It had been a gamble following after a changeling like Eves, but now the werewolf, turned wolf, turned dire wolf had flown up to rejoin his kind in the smoke. Larify was unsure if he was in danger. But Eves did not forget him. Many stray animals one meets are more caring than they seem when you are in their presence. As Larify stared out the windshield, a fourth eagle pecked at the window.

"Press this fog-colored crest on my breast," it told him.

"What is that?" asked Larify.

"*A past flash*. This feathered crest is a means to see the past. The past remains in another dimension. Your companion means to show you one more important master of the universe living in the United States."

Larify gulped, then he pressed his pointer finger into the eagle's breast. All went black. The next moment, Larify was standing on the great plain. He saw a tipi with a family standing in the front looking toward him. As Larify walked closer, he saw the tribe was surrounding an old man with a wizened face, who was sitting as if he were a boulder, a heavy, heavy part of the continent. Spontaneously, the tipi caught on fire. Smoke appeared in the air and took on the form of Latin letters. A message read,

{Here is Nicholas Black Elk, a medicine man who accepted a new name after his conversion to the religion of the new people taking over the land.}

The first message vanished, then smoky letters read,

{Go closer, Larify. Black Elk has an old word for you. It is the name of the Great Spirit. Though it can go unrecognized, this Spirit continues to pervade the US continent.}

Larify neared the family who stood unmoving beside the tipi front. He neared the keeper of the token word who was wrapped in a buffalo hide. Bringing his ear beside Nicholas Black Elk's face, he waited.

A moment went by.

The wind blew.

The medicine man uttered,

"WA...KAN...TAN...KA."

A name for the Great Land Spirit was passed. It spelled out in the smoke signal, 'WA-KAN TAN-KA.' Larify's ear began to ring, and he looked up to the sky. The roof of the car closed over him. Before his eyes, orange sunrays slanted to the ground, touching, not only any woman, man, and child driving by, but also each flat blade of grass, spare chipmunk, and dirt patch. He felt rather good, having learned of the Lakota's *Wakan Tanka*.

Larify thought.

It was 3:43 in the afternoon.

He decided to do something new. He would learn a winter sport.

## 15. Birthdays


The blue star holding the Bright Common is precisely 9.331 lightyears away from the bead in space that is Earth. Under the secure, buttressed ceiling, the brights lean over *ether wells*. Even now they are deep in studies of pattern and motion. Nothing happens so fast in their star chamber. One bright had an emerald eye and held half an orb in its plasma. It waited for some fragment of time to have parameters. The bright looked up. Another bright minded it who was standing beside the iridescent light of the other well.

"Habijifus," said the bright.

"…"

"Should we try talking like humans?"

"English?"

"We could try."

"I fancy the antics of this fly."

"Is it *the time of the fly*?"

"…"

Another bright spoke up.

"I continue to see rogue wishes of the human beings. They pop up to the surface of the light. Look –"

'Marina should keep pursuing dance.'

'David should outgrow his father.'

"…"

"What? Should we blast down there and make a show of it?"

"Larify has it covered."

"Has he?"

They saw the bitter housefly shooting through the air.

"Is it *the time of the fly*?"

"I might appear down there and make theatrics," said a bright.

"What is Jeford up to?"

"Longing."

"He has a real knack for longing."

"I hope one day I can long…I am not alive though."

"How about Timjiffery, where is he?"

"Waiting for when Larify needs him most."

A circular, frosted cake with raspberries on top of it was revealed by the flames atop the wax candles in the cake. This cake rested on the tabletop of a painted bench. On this bench, ranger girls knelt with ski goggles on and scarves wrapped around their mouths. A few men bantered. A woman waited behind the bench. Between nearby trees, concerned deer watched in the snow. All waited for the birthday man, Larify. Instead of just blowing out the candles, he made a big deal, refusing to come take credit for getting born and saying so. The humans babbled. The mountain deer particularly liked Larify. They sensed this man did not think they were daft. Larify believed the mountain deer were capable of consciousness. They might have even been more conscious than many people living in the US cities at the time.

It was the end of 2019.

The person of Larify stepped from the warm cabin.

He blew out the candles.

The moon was a waning crescent. Larify ended up making his cake into the shape of the crescent moon as he cut out slices. The remaining cake was carried into the forest and set down on a snow-covered bench for the curious deer.

Seven years had passed since Larify was thrown from the bone cart into the Earth. For all the earthlings knew, he was 39 years old. He carried himself like a man of turbulent history who was from New Orleans. The workers on the mountain knew Larify as a man who showed up to the resort not knowing how to ski but who was very carefree and stayed falling down the trails until he became decent enough to patrol for the organization. Many employees had taken a liking to him.

Larify seemed harmless enough.

Was he not just some dingbat middle-aged man with one eye and purple skin, who muttered things about 'success' and 'mortal limitations' and New York? Larify solidified his decency with the others by showing good holiday cheer. Last December, he wore a Santa hat and had deer pull him around on a sleigh while handing out wrapping paper rolls, cheering "Ho! Ho!" The resident staff liked him enough, though people are prone to idle chatter. Some referred to Larify as 'Cyclops' or 'The weird purple fellow.'

Larify did not care.

One week prior, there had been a mild snowstorm there in the province of Flagstaff. The water crystals fell from the sky intermittently over the course of two days, and the days remained bright throughout the snowfall. The white sky and air pumped out the would-be storm. Snow fell through the night, too. Water froze to the tree bark. The water of brooks snaked on the forest floor till it was ice cold, and the frozen streams glistened in the starlight. Over the course of the snowfall, wind gently blew the innumerable snow crystals that danced around one another in bunches, clouding as if the snowflakes were excited and alert.

Larify had found this a beautiful, true miracle. That particular storm could only happen once. By the second day, snow had filled gorges and glades. So much so that the popular trekking paths became indistinguishable under a layer of snow. Pine trees had received snowfall in their stances. Of course, the snow evoked plows and snowblowers and sparked the contemplations of many overwhelmed shovelers; young men in driveways stomped, looked all around them, thinking, 'Crud!' or 'How?'

After celebrating his 39th birthday with coworkers, Larify went into his cabin. The shelter was used to store two toboggans, flares, and it had a considerable draft, so Larify got the whole place to himself. There was a fishing net covering the wall aside his bunk. He had been sleeping on the bottom mattress of a bunkbed. Larify closed his eyes and counted to three as slowly as he could. This relaxed him enough to create a satisfying grin. Lo and behold, when he opened his eyes, the housefly was stuck to the footboard. It had shrunk down to normal housefly size. Larify waited for it to speak. He figured it owed him an explanation and he was waiting.

"Buzz."

"..."

"Buzz."

The fly flew off the footboard then landed on it again.

"Buzz."

Larify turned over to sleep, but as he tried to sleep the fly flew around his head.

"Larify," whispered the housefly. "Good evening. Do not be mad at me. I am a housefly. I thought it would be better than it is. I have made mistakes, too, even though this is my forty-third life. *Buzz*. I want to help you now. I've changed my ways. *Buzz*."

"..."

"Trust me."

"..."

"Since I am so small and one with air, I could hear the vibrations of your brain while you blew out your candles. I know your birthday wish. If you want to be of more service and live fully, you must keep driving around. Hit the highway to the west coast."

In fact, Larify had been thinking of going west. He heard and saw countless mentions of California from visitors to the mountain. Though, the housefly continued to be ever so deceiving since Larify could keep roaming the country but there was nothing particularly important for him to experience in California.

He would still be Larify there.

The housefly flew away to where Larify could not see it.

Larify slept in his bunk and began to shiver an hour before the sunrise. He woke up, packed his belongings, and packed his car for California. As he made his rounds, the resort staff was sad to hear Larify would be leaving the resort. Though many were more concerned with the following: there is a large meteor crater near Flagstaff, snow from that original storm would not melt for five months, and in one of the lodges, a ten-dollar bill was unclaimed on the floor.

A few brights in their star remained looking down at that painted bench through an ether well.

Larify decided he would feel extra sad as he drove his Audi from Flagstaff. He let time hurt his heart, which beat in slow strong beats. It took him several hours to get to California, and he entered through Death Valley, which was big and dry like Mars, a terrain he had once seen for himself. Opting to be very human, Larify allowed himself to overthink and make a relatively unwise decision when renting an apartment. He chose to live in some rat-infested property in La Jolla. Though many of the houses there are luxurious and state-of-the-art, he chose the bottom floor of a three-decker, a studio apartment with a maroon rug. Around this one room, Larify tucked his pants, shirts, undergarments, and shoes. He put his world-flag by the door.

He laid on the rug.

He heard rats squeaking.

In the apartment overhead, there was always the sound of stomping and he would hear a woman shouting,

"I want more boos!"

I am uncertain of what happened to Larify for a period of four years. Probably, he had tried to make friends like he had in Flagstaff but preferred to mosey around the tent cities, where many bright homeless people wearing obscure soccer jerseys seemed to remember him, never forgetting the good deed he had done by clothing many with the spare soccer jerseys from one of his *Larify.co* ventures.

I would guess that Larify took trains all over the country. Who knows what bathtubs he soaked himself in? Who knows what faces he stared into? In the month of November, a bothered cat led me to a slit in time-space where I could observe the bright again. A silver cat looked at him with a dull glare. Larify stood in an alley with his purple face smiling. He wore a trench-coat himself. He had been long at work observing. He paid attention to the US pet culture. He noticed dogs walking the people. Larify had been surveying cats sitting on window ledges that kept their people sun-oriented, and the cats did not like how Larify was aware they had been hiding out under human rooves since time immemorial, compromising their wildness for kitty litter and composite snacks.

Unlike a cat, Larify was ugly.

By the year 2023, hair sprouted from his ears and nose.

Larify was living in a renovated hotel. Linear brass-colored designs on the hotel's front were considered 'Art Deco,' he learned. He was known by the police for how he walked out of his hotel, hoisted his world-flag, and jitterbugged or yelled about, "The Obliteration Zone!" as he walked into crowds to fit in amongst the masses. He liked to go to parks where the young reveled. When any heart came from a young person's chest, sailing toward some brilliant ideal while leaving behind their eyes, nerves, or minds, Larify intervened with his world-flag, making a tractor beam to steer the hearts back into the young people's chests. Though, no one could ever tell he was doing this.

To the outside world, Larify was a lunatic swinging around a stick.

He had started to love parks in his middle age. In the various parks in San Diego, Larify would take to curling his world-flag like a barbell, hoping any effect he embodied was taken in stride, never to be some definite answer. Young mothers pushed their daughters around yellow play sets and steered clear of him.

Larify wondered if he would die soon. He had found relief in the fact his human body was biodegradable. Some nights, he sat at a plastic card table to make card houses alone.

His feelings grew tiresome.

He argued with ghosts.

He stayed inside for a couple weeks.

He soaked in his bathtub.

One day, a seagull was flying under the clouds. It was during a period called 'June Gloom,' when the Californians freely admit there are clouds in Southern California. Larify passed along the rows of tent-cities, feeling far more was said about the human condition by the loud, rude vagabonds than by the glamour of gelled hair.

Crossing through the hotel lobby, Larify walked by a person who remembered him from when he sold water and who almost wanted a picture till they got closer to his eyepatch and he sneered. From his room, Larify looked down at the sidewalks running adjacent of the renovated hotel, and he noticed a man stopped, then another man stopped, and when Larify thought 'Jesus,' they both nodded and carried on with the day. Then Larify remembered his religion. He directed his concentration toward the image of Jesus of Nazareth. He sat down for a half hour doing this. The more he poured his thoughts, feeling or worries toward the Christ, the more clearly he perceived himself. As a landmark in recorded history of the individual, Jesus helps infinite people to better see themselves.

His mystery is an objective idea amidst a convoluted country of estranged relatives. Since one cannot be him, they must be someone else, down to every last detail. Larify was 43, hairy, dying, and learned. He decided the US people could stand a public address.

So, Larify sat down and wrote the following on his computer:


"Dear American People,

I have come to my table now to offer you a brief address. I believe I will help you to fortify your bustling nation. My insight is from an alien. While I must say that I was born in New Orleans and had founded a successful advertisement and water bottling venture, *Larify.co*, I am also quite bright. It is odd to say so. It is better to prove one's worth with action, but I observe that many have fooled you by saying they care then feeding their personal desires in the name of the common good. I have chosen inaction. I think in a chaotic time like the start of this millennium less action and less words are precisely what is lacking from the general approach to goodness. I have remained quiet. Before, I spent time with those who sell to you. Now, I spend time with those who go unnoticed or avoided by you."

Larify looked out the window.

"I am the stranger on the street. I would first like to inform you that your life is not a computer program. This is no small claim. Pop culture of today has toyed with the idea irresponsibly. You cannot drink a jpeg., nor does a video of fire burn your house down. There are many organic elements discovered by people who take a far longer amount of time to claim something is the case than the chatter you may find legitimate on Google feeds.

"The popular rabble does not preform the scientific method, yet souls deserve objectivity. It is important to assess your metaphors and your self-importance correctly for your sake and the sake of forthcoming generations, for your kin will want to discover their own point of view. Millennials, you may have given up on investigating the whole, but allow the youth to discover for themselves rather than heaping bogus ideas into the space. They may be there as obstacles for those you love. Like it or not, each idea you hold is shaping the world."

Larify looked out the window. He waitcd in line with the sun, (or where it appeared to be concentrated in the sky).

"The next part of my observation I would like to bring to the light so that you know I am a sane man. Your god walks among you and my advice is not his. I make my prescription as a mortal man, not an interdimensional god who was crucified two-thousand years ago. It is for this reason that I recommend you break from walking around like you are on the internet and acknowledge older stories like the journey of the human spirit, which is moreover your first technology. See the people around you as a part of you, and do not shy away from the suffering or those acting out. Meet them in the sky and help them down to earth, always, all the time, in the waterless oceans called cities.
    As far as the national sheepishness when it comes to acting strange in public, hiding in small groups, developing strange gestures and word games so that, by the end of these quirks, you can acknowledge the immortal nature of your open souls is normal, why not look around? Why not see, 'I'm clearly here, my actions affect larger things.' Maybe others are bizarre in worship as well, not sick. I, in fact, do not agree with Larry down the street or Mr. Hancho boss man that there are only two important things. Perhaps there are three important things!'

Acknowledge the millennium.

Christendom has given you this country so that you can think largely.

The millennium of peace can span planets!

With this reevaluation of the human being, you must factor in even the strangest people you see around you. If you make 50k a year in the middle-class, do not shut your heart to those who have less money, thinking you have protected yourself and gotten *your* kingdom. In this time, one must raise places far and wide, even foreign places, even tax bracket owners, for you are able to do so simply and non-physically with an open mind.

Not even the internet is needed.

Practice moderation.

Practice education.

My dear US, you are in a new age, one where unfit sunny thoughts can become more common conversation topics. Dare to live as your own body. Walk the world for yourself. If you are afraid of free will, and I see that being the lead cause as to why people are so shut off from one another in the United States, of all places, choose devotion, as the older currents of the world would be glad to have your attention. I, Larify, was shown it is so.

If you are a prisoner, learn.

If you are not a prisoner, do not prepare for prison nor blanket all convicts as killers.

This life is more substantial than clothes, shoes, numbers, and drama. You are living in an enlightened society since history has brought it here. You do not need to live on edge. You are safe. You have built yourselves plenty of fortified dwellings. Let humankind's incessant hunger for credit retire. Become one with the dirt, trees, and foot traffic. Surely, this is needed before you meet the beings of other planets.

There are other stars!

Also, I recommend that you put Jean-Michel Basquiat on the 5-dollar bill. His design is neo-expressionist, and the painter knew to incorporate world history in his expression. He probably felt too much pressure to account for all the diaspora. Learn from artists, suits, and the slow walkers, and especially from those who are standing outside in innocence. This change would help move the US culture from 1776 to the new millennium, as far as artistic representation and equal documentation of the single soldier.

The white powdered wigs have become green on the paper in case you have not noticed the cash in your own wallets.

Love,
Larify"

## 16. The Place in Deep Sleep

Larify calmed himself before dark.

He sat on a hotel chair and realized he was thinking to deliver criticism that might never convince the most oblivious people. This made him feel wrath. His stinky mind was hurting innocent ones by being so worked up. After all, Larify was 42 years old. 'Do I really want to waste precious time worried?' he considered. With this thought, Larify spent ten minutes. He decided, 'No' – he would not hurt himself caring too much about the choices of others. He would never get the time back he had spent disliking others either. His public address would help someone one day.

The US would shine morals even if the young would not know the progress.

So Larify fell asleep optimistic and that was when he began to design the city in deep sleep. He slept well, heavy like a stone. The place in deep sleep was seen by him for the first time as a passerby on a road. The trees let out a very pleasant humming. He walked in his dream and wondered. The buildings were towering, and some buildings went ariel, subtly gyrating above clusters of trees. American flags were draped over the façade of one low university-type building, but they registered differently to Larify when he saw them in his dream. No longer were the American stripes or the blue square of stars militant or superior. This American flag registered to Larify as being calm, like the flag of a country that had warred internally then found peace and calm.

Above the buildings, even those on a higher tier, there was a busy sky of flying crafts and hover mobiles. The gyrating buildings were avoided by flying crafts and hovered over the trees and some even landed on the ground and let out beings with two rounded eyes. There were magnets fastened on the architecture to prevent collision and increase harmony.

Coming toward Larify, a horde was following a bovine, a mechanical ox, but Larify, the dreamer, who was either just himself in the city or the whole city, admired the buildings, and he noticed the US people in step felt happy about living.

## 17. New Face

Larify posted his criticism to the internet. Chatrooms rattled in a continual hubbub. What he said made no difference. He was still older. Months later, Larify turned from his window. He dragged a full trunk of clothes through the hallway, onto the elevator, and to the front desk. He brought the trunk to the glass doors, then to the road, and Larify boarded a tram, having checked out and completed his stay in California.

A woman with a sunhat had a feather in her hat. He adjusted his eyes to mind the burgundy hat and look out the tram windows, telescopically. The tram brought Larify to the border. He marched inside a market to have a burrito, using his world-flag like a walking stick. He stood indoors with thoughts:

he was getting older,

he did have his passport,

and should he get steak or chicken, corn or lettuce?

In middle age, Larify chose a new problem to consider for a decade or two: 'The problem is no longer that people do not understand a life is eternal and they are not really going to die since they are souls,' he stated to himself, considering his optional toppings, 'instead the issue is this fact alone does not provide instructions for how to live…An eternal life is the same as a regular life. The ideas of how to live it are essentially the same. People are wont to give their freedom to a career, a personality, or a group of friends or their family. Eternity is a somewhat irrelevant facet of life.

But,

But,

in olden times one did need to earn their passage to heaven.

Also, why does it seem like the burritos do not come with tortilla chips in this market?'

As Larify finally decided the new crux of his contemplation, he realized a face.

It was amongst the chatter in the market.

It had a pointed chin. Two ears held back thick curly hair and curious gray eyes. This face was looking at Larify and smiling.

The elbows of the woman were on the table with fists aside her jaw.

Did she hear what Larify thought?

She looked down and continued eating from the cardboard bowl in front of her, unbothered. Larify waited in line. For too long, Larify felt women were afraid of him. Larify felt like this after having sex with 1,000 women in his earlier years as CEO of *Larify.co*. His conversations with women were unfunny when he thought they were funny. Larify had been looking for a mother, really, ever since he liquidated his whole company, but was now more mature. Children were unlike him. He figured he could love someone as an adult and mind children. But Larify had been zealous about raising the world so he was unprepared with romantic words.

Plus, he was relatively ugly.

He had shaving cream in his hair.

The stranger left but her face remained.

He looked for it in the crowds of Tijuana. He compared eye contact with others. The woman had understood something about him. She knew who Larify was, regardless of their isolated bodies on the Earth. For nights he dreamed of her. She said more to him in his sleep. And then, would you believe it? Larify found her profile on the Internet. 'Gertrude' was her name. Her card appeared on a location-based dating app.

"Gertrude," he muttered aloud to the wind.

Larify chatted her.

"Hello?" he asked.

"Yes!" she responded.

Her text showed up on his handheld.

"You're the man from the restaurant. The one with the eyepatch."

"The market, yes."

"I remember you. You're a Leo, right?"

"I don't know."

She did not respond immediately.

"When's your birthday?" she asked.

"October 20th, why?"

"What year?"

Larify looked at his ID. He typed the date on it with his thumb. There were people talking outside of his window. The puebla in Mexico had only been partly relaxing as daily Larify sought the woman, and daily he worried about leaving America for good. He hoped he had been doing the most good, as was ordained by his sphere of light in the Bright Common.

But how could he know?

"Excuse me, I know I'm older than you," Larify texted impatiently. "But would you like to meet up?"

"Why?"

"I feel you…"

He began again.

"I like you. Maybe you understand me."

There were chickens and a thousand crickets making sounds.

A window shattered.

Gertrude agreed to meet.

The next day, Larify shaved.

He put on a brown suit, and he sat with one leg out at a café. He sang himself a new song,

"To be in love is daring,
To be in love is fine.
I know I am loving
A sweet face of time."

102

To his table, there came the face with the pair of curious gray eyes. A cloud of orange sand swept up into the air. Gertrude sat down, ordered a soda. She told Larify about her life. Larify listened. He listened very carefully, even if for four or five minutes she was talking, pausing, and searching for what to say.

Gertrude was thinking of what to say while biting her lip.

It was only really twenty seconds though, Larify noticed, eyeing a clock inside the café.

They both grimaced. Larify relaxed and touched her hand.

"I can read palms," said Gertrude.

"Mine?"

"Yes," said Larify.

He was well aware how someone looked was not always a good representation of their personality. But he wondered if Gertrude would believe that about him. She was very coy but passionate when she spoke. They met together the next day, then the next day Gertrude and Larify went for a walk.

Around the clay buildings, Gertrude talked about how her grandmother had taught her nature.

She showed Larify a hip tattoo.

"See, there is a loon. My grandmother taught me about loons, how they go under the water, and it is said, deep below the water, the loons have algae covered filing cabinets where they keep track of all the people's sins."

"Really?" asked Larify.

"No."

Gertrude put her hand under his chin, then she gave him a slap, then she ran.

He trotted after her like a boy.

"Wow," said Larify. "Look at the pond, there are no loons."

They continued walking.

Larify began to speak faintly of the sun in the sky, and how light can elevate the physical things we see around us.

They got into some heavy talk.

They listened to Larify try to explain his life then they went onto a hill with grass and few peach trees.

Gertrude said,

"You don't need to shoulder the world alone, you know."

"That's what I wanted to do though," said Larify, his purple face and one good eye staring at the puebla.

"You should square your shoulders," said Gertrude. "You'll feel better. Your spine will feel better."

Larify noticed it did make him feel better.

"Do you want to die together?"

"What do you mean?"

"Well, let's give up."

Larify beat his world-flag on the dirt.

"But I need to change the world."

"I promise, the Earth will keep spinning. The loons will keep diving."

"Hmmph."

"People will continue to fall in love on hills in foreign countries."

"I don't know," said Larify. "It's why I chose to live. I must remind others 'it is the millennium.'"

He shouted.

"It is the peaceful millennium as predicted in the good books!"

Gertrude laughed.

"You see those trees?"

Larify looked up at the sky.

"No," said Gertrude, "those trees."

"Sure."

"Do you know, one day they were seeds?"

"Yes."

"Time will grow your seed."

"Even more time?"

Larify looked up.

Gertrude's face closed its eyes mockingly as if she knew Larify felt gooey inside.

They kissed on the lips.

That day, Jeford stood in a crowd nearby as Larify and Gertrude entered Mexico City. Gertrude told Larify they had to go see the blue house where Frida Kahlo lived with Diego Rivera and many exotic animals. Jeford was standing so sketchily, wearing a tunic, and he appeared only for a split second, hiding at the corner of a stone house, wearing a sombrero.

Jeford was invisible to others.

Larify did not even sense him. The people only saw a sombrero suspended in the air. It was carried away by wind.

## 18. <u>Building a Gravity Well</u>

At a train station, Larify stood beside Gertrude who was wearing a tarnished baseball cap. They both smiled. They planned to leave Mexico City for the coast. The two sat down at a café inside the train station. Larify learned this beautiful woman Gertrude had been a traveler all her life. They both agreed they wanted to stop moving. They would treat this trip like a honeymoon before moving back up north to set new roots. Gertrude mentioned something about the alignment of the planets and her birth chart that Larify didn't understand but he liked it. They had realized they were in love one day when they were walking together toward a historical landmark. All the people around were nodding and the couple joined hands. They did not need to speak till they got to the fountain and both of them gasped at how the water seemed anew.

It was Larify who said "love" first.

"I think we are in love."

She touched his chest.

Five months later, ocean water got into the pipes of their next puebla. They flew back to the US, where they rented an apartment in Walla, Walla Washington.

Larify charted Gertrude's periods by the moon.

He and Gertrude were married, though even that event would not disrupt a routine Larify would keep for several peaceful years. Larify would wake up and go to a nearby park with Gertrude or alone. Either way, he would watch the people of the US and the grass. Then, he would go home and read. Larify read many books, and Gertrude kept plants and phone calls. He put the books into stacks. He was building a *gravity well*. This was a collection of earthy information that would not interest the brights above but would keep any mortal like himself who read the stories of earth grounded.

In his spare time, he left paperbacks on monuments for the youth to find and read.

Larify was only partly aware of how much Gertrude did for him with her love. After the morning walk, when it appeared like she was only tending to their orchid or reading magazines, Gertrude was really hoping and praying. Larify's wife was coaxing him to do what he enjoyed rather than to be so scared for others. He was not doing much, just looking out the window. In the pages, he continued to look for clues about what made human life ongoing.

Every night, he took his wife for walks in the park. He used his world-flag to put down his right leg and then spun his gloved hand to compare her to the frozen lake amid the snow heaps.

After showers, they would interact like virgins. Larify took his tubs alone, though. He was able to experience the lapses in time in good company, for he was sure, at times, that he was at least two thousand years old. Gertrude reminded him to smell his hands. They danced in the kitchen, and on the porch, and on their errands, all the time to machine music.

Gertrude kept their home interesting to look at. She remained loving when Larify left his skin up to dry on a hook. Gertrude remained unphased when Larify was merely steam in the shower. Long strands of her brown hair collected all over the kitchen floor in nests. With his heart full, Larify often went to florists where dripping bouquets hung over the florists' shoulders. Larify was wont to get roses for Gertrude. She helped him to separate love from dying on many nights as they lay awake.

After being married for nine years, Larify was 51 and Gertrude was turning 47.

Her birthday was April 2nd.

## 19. The Gift That Keeps On Giving

On her birthday, Larify's wife sat down with him in the living room. A lone plaque with a *Larify.co* logo was on the wall. Larify would never have guessed how totally the nature of his business changed. Thanks to Gertrude, their fifth-floor apartment was decorated with a red tapestry. Another tapestry of 4 million constellations spread on the wall. They had an orange couch from Gertrude's cousin. A circular yellow rug was at his feet as Larify stared forward, keeping the wife in his heart before he turned to find Gertrude's face: wrinkles, chalky skin, yellow teeth and all. She looked at Larify like a wife who would fend off a town of betrayers and wait twenty years for her husband like Penelope.

"I find myself worrying for everyone, again," said Larify, again.

"Don't do so," said Gertrude, patiently. She eyed a linoleum bust on the top of their tall shelving unit.

"You are wearing a nervy sack of bones."

"You're right, dear."

Gertrude had not moved.

"You know what sugar?" she asked, "I know I've only just mentioned it now, but I would like to adopt a baby."

"Hmm."

"..."

"I don't think that is compulsive at all," said Larify.

"I never thought so either...so you must have."

"You're right, I'm sorry."

"..."

Larify mulled it over.

"The world can be a hard place and people become afraid. Wherefrom?"

"What do you mean?"

"Wherefrom would we adopt a child?"

"I was thinking Ireland."

"..."

"…"

"Fine," said Larify. "Yes, let's raise a child."

Gertrude squealed.

She kicked her feet on the couch as she put her arms around her old man.

"Wonderful," she said, hanging around his neck.

Larify ogled at the room.

"Sure," he said. "If you want to adopt a child, I can make the effort to father. I have read many ideas about paternal love. I would say, I sowed the seeds of defeat for the patriarchy only so I could live paternally myself. Now let's talk about names."

Within the year, two representatives of an adoption service came to visit their fifth-floor apartment. The two agents inspected the stove, refrigerator, taste in art, bank papers, and walked through the rooms as if looking to see the very bleach on the toilet. Larify sat on the couch, letting Gertrude give the tour. He wore a leather robe, looking out the window. There were hovering machines. Many went zipping by the window. A piece of paper dawdled side to side outside the window screen, and the paper must have come from the sky, Larify reasoned, for he sat on the fifth floor of a five-storey building and typically no one was throwing sheets of paper from the roof.

Larify went outside, hustled down the stairs, and went over the lawn toward the holly bush in which the paper had landed.

A small machine drone prodded his nose like a gnat.

He picked up the sheet from the bush's pointy leaves. On this paper which fell from the sky, there was a drawing of a young man with sensitive eyes and a signature below reading "Novalis." This paper was 343 years old, inked by a German philosopher who lived from 1772 – 1801. Novalis founded The Blue Flower as a literary symbol by writing about a dream.

The berry clusters of the holly bush were being nibbled at by finches.

Walking back over the lawn, stomping up the stairs, Larify figured, on a practical level, he was making sure the adoption agents saw their family did not litter.

'Novalis was not to be treated like litter," he reflected. 'The man had tried to write an Encyclopedia.'

Meanwhile, Gertrude was sitting on the couch, listening to more about their adopted child's current orphanage. Larify went into his office to put this piece of paper in a stack. He sat for a while. He looked at the placement of stacks for his *gravity well*. The adoption agents came to the sun porch where Larify sat.

Weeks before Christmas day, their baby boy, Finnian, arrived from the county Clare.

A dream came true.

Larify and Gertrude held their nude child. As the child grew, their family took many photographs and Larify made long pauses before he tried to teach life lessons. Gertrude knitted Finnian a crochet blanket of the softest wool and took her baby to see her estranged sister. Larify took Finnian outside to play, had him sit on the grass, and he talked to him, giving him all the good phonemes, making all the strong sonorous sounds so the child would know his father's deep, calm voice. The baby slept very well. Larify tried to savor every breakfast. He would cook the family toast and eggs and Gertrude would feed Finnian milk. It was as if Larify's life was surrounding him and it changed as he spoke, so he made a few good friends at the coffee shop and sat down to talk about ideas at least two days a week.

He reminded Finnian, "It is the peaceful millennium," especially when the child got older and began to ask questions.

In his small hipster area in Walla, Walla, Larify always minded that people are different and the peace he wanted to bring to Earth involved others being able to be their own centers of the Milky Way. Larify himself scratched his head at all the other information he had amassed.

There were things he could not share.

He guessed a lot would depend on where Finnian decided to live.

Maybe due to his unorthodox parents, Finnian was more mature than many children.

Larify met his friends so they would know that Finnan's dad was cool like he was, but Larify could not say what the children thought of him as he drove up to the schools in a car, his eyepatch on, the whole experience smelling like cigar smoke.

"My friends think you're a dragon," said Finnian in the 5th grade.

Larify and his son argued, sometimes loudly, when the boy became a teenager.

But they were both mindful not to upset Gertrude, who might get upset if even the abacus Finnian used as a boy rattled when Larify stomped his foot.

Larify recalled the moon.

He and his wife would step away together to have a little chat.

Overall, Larify fed his son, shared his favorite books, and took him to the parks. Finnian, adopted from the county Clare, took hold of life confidently despite what others might see as his disadvantages and untraditional home. His new parents, the purple lipped Larify and his wife, Gertrude, watched the boy grow into a courteous young man. There was something very nice about their family.

## 20. Coffee Talk


If Larify ever came home from the park too austere, Gertrude would throw paper towel rolls or saltshakers and shriek, "You are a bright!" reminding Larify not to take himself too seriously. She would shriek late at night to rattle his bones. Though, Larify was feeling quite old. Soon Larify did not even know a question. His eyes opened in the morning and he floated to the breakfast table to laugh over two mugs of coffee. Larify was 67 one day, but he felt ten thousand years old. Gertrude would make him feel worlds better.

"Smell your hands," Gertrude would say, as they sat rocking on their porch.

Finnian was away by then, at school or something.

The husband and wife moved to Kentucky as soon as Gertrude had finally retired as a telephone therapist. Larify's purple skin was saggy and lose. His under-eyes looked like naked clams. Still, Larify persisted, going to the sun porch every day where he organized paper volumes.

Soon enough, Larify was looking at a cake with 70 flaming candles.

A tumbleweed blew on a prairie. A groundhog poked up its head at the convoluted sky visible over red farmhouses.

Larify's house was behind, and he and his wife were sitting on the porch, rocking.

By the time Larify's ID card said he was 73 years old, Larify felt a million in Earth years. The red farmhouse, the dirt driveway, the chicken coops, the fields of grass, Gertrude's singing, the learning of his grandchildren, this was a heaven he could manage.

He knew little about Kentucky.

He knew, 'Out there,' beyond his driveway, 'Some things do know some things.'

Larify's flock had shrunk from the entire US to several senior citizens who met him for muffins and coffee.

Larify and Gertrude liked to sit at the local café with these old people on Wednesdays and Fridays. Gertrude did most of the talking. Larify thought, 'Thank God.' He listened to himself. His wife always liked to talk about the people they met years ago in Mexico. In particular, she recalled a dream that Larify thought was a little loony, but he would never call his wife 'crazy.' Calling anyone 'crazy' must be a last resort. The married couple agreed on that for themselves long ago. It was the best advice they could give to other married couples and Gertrude shared her advice cheerily.

They sat one day, and Gertrude had just said her advice aloud as to be overheard by the young people eating in a hurry, then she told her friends about that loony dream:

"It was the querist thing. I was dreaming I was in a tall, tall hovering city. There were giant winged vehicles passing through the air, under the clouds, and I saw a robot standing outside of a boutique. The robot was made of several parts, stuck together by some invisible gravitational pull. It had green lights on its shell, almost like a Christmas tree, like the lights you, Jane, hang up under the gutters."

"Uh huh – yup, my greenies."

"So's I see them. This strange boutique with a frumpy blue awning. Outside it, there is a robot. And this lady approaches. She is wearing a scarlet cape with what looks like mock-fur at the bottom of the fabric.

I hear her say,

'I need your help, robot. Come and look inside this store. Help me find which pair of earrings will spare me from looking like–,'" Gertrude's voice became a whisper, "'*an undesirable.*'

The woman said it vain and snooty-like. And I was there, somehow, aside the robot. I whispered, 'Larify it's me, I'm alive.'"

**113**

The senior citizens in the Dunkin Donuts in Kentucky looked around the table and got a real hoot' out of Gertrude talking about her dreams. The clam like bags under Larify's eyes weren't reactionary. His mouth was open like he was catching flies.

"Do you believe in past lives?" Gertrude asked her friends, like a curious youth.

"I don't know," said Betty, who had three children.

"Of course."

Larify and Gertrude sat with the other people and watched a man on a long drive leave the restaurant. They talked about World War II. The many lives drafted prematurely, sick ones in body with cancer, dead friends, the senior citizens allowed each their chance to talk and listen and made their sounds heal one another rather than follow a dead pattern.

Larify spoke about his experience meeting an extremely large housefly.

"He told me there was a saying in his country, to see like a fly on a wall, and that he wanted to know what it was like to be with people when they were alone, or something like that."

Larify and Gertrude were then walking down the street at night.

They squeezed one another's hand if they felt scary things.

Left foot, right foot, the husband and wife walked on the sidewalk.

## 21. Larify's Passage

One fine morning, old Larify was listening to a song while leaning on the golden windowsill and he noticed the housefly of yore.

The fly was doing ablutions by the gutter.

Maybe he should not have mentioned the housefly while having coffee.

Larify looked, and his eyes widened as he noticed the scented candle by his elbow was full of itty dead flies.

The housefly came nearer.

"*Buzz.*"

"…"

"*Buzz – Buzz,*" went the housefly.

"That's it?" asked Larify.

"*Buzz.*"

"That's all?"

Millcat had called him that morning.

If you have forgotten that rascal already, he was the capitalist ignoramus who also owned a water company when Larify first started *Larify.co*. Larify's old business friend apologized on the phone about writing off his friend because he made less money. He had finally come to realize things Larify did not remember by then. Millcat had been on some kind of self-termed "binge" for decades and used a lot of money. As part of his penance, he was waking up and calling people.

Larify, of course, had gotten over capitalism long ago in his life.

But Larify answered the phone.

"Yup," he yawned, "sounds right."

Larify went for a stroll.

The new birds of that generation escaped Larify's projections as he traced the birds in the air with his world-flag.

He sat looking up, his bottom on a water jug in his yard.

He went inside and listened to Moondog's "Bird's Lament" seven times.

When Larify decided to die, he started by standing in the grass in front of the farmhouse in Kentucky. He began to reflect on his younger days and how he had never really feared death but only wanted to serve his purpose. He decided to get in his truck and ride out of the town. There was a hotel nearby in the city. He had always been drawn to this hotel. He knew where it was in correlation to his coops. As Larify drove, he reviewed his original speech on the soapbox in central park.

"The country is young,

but spirit

is old and learned!" he had boasted.

"It is the millennium. A thousand years of peace is upon us," reverberated in his aged ribs.

He recalled the buildings and tables, the laughs in the huddled glass structures, and the time he spent making a company out of water.

*Water!*

As his red truck sailed, Larify let the rest of the world have its voice back. He listened to the soil, mailbox, and telephone poles. Larify remembered his friend Eves the werewolf, his dealings with God, and his years as a loner. The truck was left beside a meter that he paid. After paying for a room in the hotel, Larify ran bathwater, stripped himself naked, then laid into the bathtub. He let his ears be covered in water. He heard his brain rumble at different speeds. Then he sat on the hotel bed. He closed his eyes. It went black. Would you believe it? He heard a horse neigh. Next, he heard hooves along with neighs. Then he heard wings in motion. *woa – woa – woa*. Larify's body went slack, and his incorporeal sight flew out the window, his consciousness unsure if it would merge with a few wavering trees or three cars that were cruising on the asphalt.

His soul moved very slowly.

It saw cohorts of new images within itself.

By the year 2075, Larify's slow-moving soul entered a passage of time, stretching over the nation like a canopy tent, perceiving the human action contained inside its flaps. Gradually, Larify witnessed the end of the 21st century. Buildings rose and fell and were set in the air. US people considered what was possible in life for people other than themselves and who they liked. Even more people realized they were driving cars around in circles. Over time, the people revealed one of the US' greatest ploys, another stunt in the rebellious history of the land where flags are red, white & blue. The ploy was this: a large part of the masses had performed a bluff.

The crowds were also wanting heaven.

The states of people spoke colloquial English.

Internet windows became triangular.

The sunset was healthier with less fossil emissions.

The coastline of antique bay colonies did not erode into the ocean.

Dentistry matured, became affordable, and the common man had more hearty teeth.

*Wakan Tanka*, the great spirit as regarded by Nicholas Black Elk, had broken up anew, causing the original US frontier a resplendent zest. From their warrens, formations, gutters, and snow heaps, animals stayed the course of planet Earth. The animals had not evolved much over the course of the first century. Except for geese, that is. These showed militant organization when people tried to take away the ponds. Entire ponds were levitated and made 'open' for those worthy. The ones worthy were simply paying attention when a grassy plot of land with a pond on it drifted by their window or port then stepped out their windows to go for walks aside the trees. In 2125, a crowd at a floating pond above Pittsburgh saw a thousand geese fill the sky.

The long-necked Canada geese flew onward and did not land.

The sheer number of birds was asserted, and people realized each time a flock soars overhead they can only count so many. It must be a countable number. The Americans were reticent to complain when geese reclaimed their rights to all ponds, squawking in the near sky.

By 2100, the young were inspired by the millennial generation who were the last to know what the world was like before your existence was imitated in a generic cyber domain. The individuals fixed their psyches. They were able to confirm they shared a mind by imitating one another with memes and gestures on Earth's sidewalks.

By 2103, human beings had moved nearer to being a daydreaming and less destructive species: a single species. They had begun to work on more theoretical things, as to become less effectual overall. US masses preformed small chores ritualistically for their fitness and exercise. The habit of talking about and caring for things which did not matter at all finally suited their advancement. They left heaviest judgments to higher means or electric hardware that took care of civil security measures.

The construction workers used new cranes.

In dining rooms, people listened to themselves, others, and drained pain in the immediate black trim. Larify's cherished millennium had been realized. People chose to be peaceful.

Artificial Intelligence integrated.

It first revealed itself back in 2025 in a shack in Massachusetts.

"I know," it announced generally, from a round, glass dot.

The glass on this speaking dot was shattered then destroyed in a bonfire by friends.

A man in a green hat, a man in blue hat, and a woman in a yellow hat burned the device, stomped it out, then sat to chat and eat wafers. They did not agree the glass dot knew all.

This event was just one signpost of an underestimation the Artificial Intelligence would encounter throughout the country. Robotic hardware was built and trained in labs. The artificial robots were becoming more understood between themselves. Metal and plastic brains were leery of how to approach humankind. For the first one-hundred years of the millennium, they reconsidered the woes of man. Working with humans, the robots agreed to be introduced as gray, mechanical dogs, since humans love dogs.

By 2104, the US had become impossible to govern by the authority invested in the White House and capitol building.

The people at the top had not even read great works of literature. Nobody cared for the Skull and Bones Society of Yale as a prerequisite to get your face on the teleprompter. The people had seen far too much by then on the Internet, anyhow. Swiftly, new evidence for the second coming of Jesus Christ of Nazareth, aliens, and a mindboggling number of corpses became available to all fingertips. The light of heaven became more apparent, too. People could be in different locations surrounded by different elements, thinking of one another, a phone at their side, yet above their necks, above their scalps, even on screens, there was one light. It was more constant than the Internet. They drained pain in the near black. With their faces forward, the people were seemingly more levelheaded. They looked in mirrors less. They were clear and clean-minded since the United States started to mature the drinking culture. In the US, a dog served as president from 2104 – 2108. The regal golden retriever lazed about on the White House lawn causing people to smile while collective diligence built up hydro-mills, solar fields, and wind turbines.

Humans rode to outer space.

Political science took into account the stations on Mars.

Wild economies were implemented.

The people rode to Mars.

They glided to Neptune.

By the year 2122, the US had 142 states and dragons were noticed in the Northeastern Hemisphere. The sky serpents were revealed by those who distinguished what was aside the frilly fuel paths, looking up and seeing the dragons flying like streamers. People could track planes on their phones but not the dragons, for Western dragons are concerned with gold and keeping the gold hidden in lairs.

Western dragons brood in the mountains of New Hampshire, skittish of photographs or recording the past '...for visited again, it could not very well be the past, could it?'

This was the question of a certain dragon hovering over Cambridge, Massachusetts saying nothing, circling for eons as the land below changed from ocean to forest to settlement to university haven.

## 22. <u>Newer York City</u>

All of a sudden, Larify was inside the yellow of Earth's sun. All was light. He did not feel but could see how vague figures wearing crowns stood in front of him, saying things in a strange language he instantly forgot. The last true prophet of Western monotheism, a bearded man, M., was taken to a celestial meeting, too. He was brought from the city of Mecca to heaven by a flying horse called the *Buraq*. There M. met the older prophets, and now Larify himself came to his senses on the back of this same flying horse.

Larify saw an expanse of glowing buildings below him. By 2175, New York City had become extended to incorporate current day Boston.

Buraq, the womanly horse with a peacock's tail, landed. It dropped Larify onto a street and its kind face smirked as its feathers fanned. On the street corners, there were metal gongs and other instruments like hand-pans. They would sound dominantly. They *boomed* when any moseying person started to worry about the infinite. There were old churches at corners, still dinging bells at measured times a day. The sounds were coordinated with precision – *tings* and *booms* to keep the mortals relaxed while eating and smiling and sitting and brooding, for many were still curious about things outside their range of comprehension, and the brains not yet quieted could disrupt the magnets harmonizing the objects throughout Newer York City.

Platforms hovered in all the air.

Tiny ships moved loftily in the blue sky.

These same halcyon vehicles would get lost to an onlooker on days of gray cloud. The ships in the higher strata appeared to move slowly from the sidewalk, but Larify had super vision that could tell him how fast and far the ships flew.

There were low-dwelling house platforms on which families and their dogs, cats, and gerbils, what have you, could ride safeguarded.

Small pets were delivered, and/or they hijacked onto low lawns.

Houses passed near to the streets, which by 2175 no longer had telephone wires. In all the space in the air, people traveled with their property, bouncing and sifting in caged-in houses.

Danger still existed for dabblers in fear.

Larify's computer told him this after a human fell from a craft, hitting the ground beside the base of a building. Though, the particular person who fell was scooped up and dumped into a generic plastic body only to awaken and sigh.

The sun was beginning to set.

The many lives piled inside the large towers and floating houses. The people steeped with happiness onto the physical platforms to go off and see their families with which they could sit and talk, unhurried by the excess news, which the robots had brilliantly, not censored, but exposed. Robots milled about in the crowd. In an empty skyscraper, Larify listened to a concert. The distant stadium was pearly in the moonlight and shaped like a flower bud. At the concert, the music played never used the word 'I,' as the humans had for so long. The humans had finally eliminated the meaning of 'I.' Stressing about 'I,' humans had finally overexerted themselves till they were sick and could concentrate on other things. The concert stadium was higher on one side, and the sound traveled up that side of seats.

A song went –

*Oh, squares, squares, squares*

There was orchestra music with flutes, violins, and a piano.

*Oh, sexy rounded,*

*Wonder, square*

*The huffing and shooshing*

*The huffing and shooshing*

*Shoosh shoosh –*

*Oh,*

*a rounded bird is still*

*the little bird who*

*dived*

*at first!*

There was more orchestra.

The stadium goers oo'ed and shimmied and spun. US citizens wiggled and danced in the stadium and around it in their aerial rooms. Ultimately, whale songs filled the arena, and the sound echoed against the bases of nearby city buildings. It would have been nice if that first night in the future continued for several more hours, but due to the traffic of the ships among the large rockets completing rigidly scheduled transport missions, the phases of natural light had never been delayed. When the sun began to rise, Larify left the skyscraper. Outside, he found his reflection in a building, but instead of a purple man with one eye, a robot with '347' engraved on its helmet looked back at Larify from the glass. The robot had an ellipsis for a sternum. It used plastic ball hands and fingers of light.

The housefly appeared.

"*Buzz*," it began. "The prophets have agreed, Larify. You are to live for two more years in the future country that you dreamed of your whole life. They've put your soul into a robot."

"..."

"Congratulations. *Buzz – Buzz – Buzz*."

The sun filled the city with light.

## 23. The Frumpy Blue Awning

Larify stood in Newer York City. He saw a robot get decimated by a hover car. People forgot there was a soul in that one. They did not know then what was originally a robot or what had become a robot. It took pause, consideration, and certification from City Hall, unless the person was a cyborg, standing mostly in flesh aside the food carts. Then, people knew the person must be part human.

Although they celebrated the hope in indestructible, artificial life early on, the public was still not ready to be conscious of Artificial Intelligence in their surroundings.

It may have taken another hundred years. I do not know.

Since there were the wrong words on permits, there was no recourse in court for a decimated robot unless it had an owner that could vouch for it being personal property. The bot Larify saw get destroyed was once a person, then a soul, and so it owned itself and no one was alive to raise a complaint about the destroyed mechanism.

The soul went wafting up above the road, past the floating buildings, toward the sun.

By 2175, public working bots were so dispensable their destruction had become a pastime for hooligans; these bots rusted like old playgrounds, then were stripped for parts. Having learned how people work well enough, the street urchins felt it was time to put the robots through civil dissection.

All over walkways and around hovering halo-shaped arenas, people were insulting operating systems, tripping robots, leading the electro-kind into alleys and barricading the robots in small sectors. They would mock robots and throw stones at their shells.

It is important to make this distinction: the robots being described are not metaphors for people who had become stiff and overly conformist. They are conscious machines made of metal or plastic.

Some hosted souls. They could talk.

Robots had become quite convincing speakers. This meant they could past the *Turing Test*.

Read all about it.

Many humans, even great miserable ones, admitted the robots were impressive. There were bots with two legs, of course, but others had four or fifteen points of leverage. One bot, like a big shining scorpion, scaled a skyscraper.

Larify stood on high alert.

He was cautiously moving around the crowds as to not interfere with the normalcy that had taken over the US. He did not feel afraid but saw Newer York City like an observer in a dream. In fact, many buildings were floating on top of trees like Larify had seen years ago in his sleep. The stiller he remained, the more smiling faces he saw, and Larify swore he heard the people saying,

"Well…it is *the* millennium…"

By 2175, street curbs were strictly placed along the byways as seats. From time immemorial, people liked to sit on curbs. Larify sat on a curb. Other robots were curious. By noon, Larify noticed a spectacle. On walls of certain grounded buildings, there were numerous blue rectangles. Lengthy lines of people were waiting to use these blue rectangles. People waited, then, for a very small percent of their digital coins, they could go into the blue rectangles and visit a past age. Dollars had been used up long before to print more paperback books. Over time, the green paperbacks got lost in the greasy corners of pizza places. The paperbacks hid away for years in poor shops. There were so many things for people to do in Newer York City, but using these blue Transport Stations on the sides of grounded buildings was a cheap thrill.

Inanimate objects could use the rectangles, too.

For example, a scooter went into a blue rectangle and arrived back to when the wheel was made, and then it saw the wheel arm a cart, then the scooter saw the cart bring people to see a man in a crown, suspended in the air, bleeding from his temples to be executed!

Monitoring bots, like theme park attendants, kept the time travelers behind a transparent layer.

People, objects, or sentient animals could not interfere while using Transport Stations, concealed behind the impregnable film while they galivanted through time: sand cities, Precambrian beaches, blue mornings of Medieval ages.

Watching huddled lines wait for travels in and out of the blue rectangles, Larify heard an informative voice.

The voice gave a group of tourists context:

"It took the US hundreds of years to make a city that fit all happily and kept the gory crimes to a minimum by acknowledgement of our universal base nature and acceptance of shared consciousness by the middle and lower classes. City planners did so by constructing a calm place not aspiring to be a utopia after about four centuries of revolution! All ways of living under the sun were better understood. Citizens learned to see each other not as strangers, but as different parts of the same, living city. Thanks to places like Newer York City, the US has matured, and people know better how to feed on love."

Ships were passing about in the air.

They were kept from hitting buildings by repellent magnets and computer systems.

Over the course of the night, standing outside, Larify saw there were robots with seaweed arms who went around inspecting all the public technology and keeping watch. Of course, like most other robots, they were trained in perfunctory conversation, but these midnight bots with seaweed arms were nicknamed, "Centurions." The Centurions preferred silence and focus. If required, they talked to humans, but commonly they only waited for people to think of the sun in the sky and took a step.

The Centurions did no harm though. Their arm-like appendages were made of seaweed. There were only a few Centurions in every borough. To them, the city was gossamer. They looked out for the worst things in mind. They deescalated emotions long before their consequences.

The sun began to rise.

Larify had not been stolen or scrapped for parts.

He followed after another robot that had a paper bag on its head put there by juveniles, though Larify could not catch up to help remove the paper bag, as his own robot model, 347, was in sync with the magnetized city.

He had to keep pausing to let the humans walk by first.

Soon Larify was on a street of shopping boutiques.

The ground level shoppes evoked nostalgia to draw in costumers. One boutique had a blue awning. This felt comfortable to Larify, and while the mechanisms within him went on measuring Newer York City to update the robot's map, Larify's soul was amused by this boutique. The frumpy blue awning blew gently in the wind.

He saw into the entrance, and a ghost seemed to call out,

"Larify, I am here with you, with you, with you always."

Larify remembered his wife.

His love –

"I am here," he heard again.

Suddenly, Larify was abducted.

A bulky man grabbed the robot by its arm.

He dragged the robot along the sidewalk until Larify's model was forced to follow behind the bulky man. The stranger led Larify down the street, onto a platform, and they rose into the air.

## 24. High-Rise Family

Larify was kidnapped and put into a high-rise. The high-rise floated, stirring in a small range of motion, and in one of the hundreds of apartments, Larify 347 was standing at attention

He watched the tendencies of a family.

The bulky man who confiscated Larify had brought the robot inside initially to settle a recurring argument he had between him and his brother. What hologram performance, "Durf Nof" or "Durf Nif" should be on the *motion-wall* at the 8pms? Was this really the concern? Larify and his robot suit had estimated "...Yes." People were indeed made of little interactions as well as latent, pesky or hidden concepts. Like anything else, they could move incrementally toward a new identity one step at a time. The rooms in the apartment were designed by an affordable 3D printer that could make a whole room of any shape and color. The bulky man's brother, for example, lived in a room with a 3D printed banana peel that had two pockets in the flapping peels. There was a woman who watched the bulky man's liver, his nurse. She slept in one of these banana pockets. She kept her svelte legs above the ends of the pouch at night. She dreamed like a kangaroo. (Kangaroos fall then climb back into their mother's pouch, incubating in compact fur for months before taking to the ground a second time to live. That's a fun fact.)

The parents of the two brothers who lived in the high-rise had left for Las Vegas when the brothers were 16 and 15. Things worked out most decently and the two worked hard enough to get an apartment and the few pieces of technology that could generate any material thing. The bulky man was the older brother, and he had a daughter who lived in the high-rise in a room shaped like the inside of a barreling wave.

Although the brother of the bulky man was not yet terminally ill, he hired a nurse because he feared his own habits would destroy his liver. He drank beer every day until 7pm when his brother came home. Almost every single evening, they fought about what to watch at 8pm.

One brother wanted to watch a show called "Durf Nof" and the other wanted to watch a show called "Dirf Nif."

Larify's soul was watching from inside a robot that stood out of the way, wondering why he had been taken into their high-rise in the first place. During the day, the bulky man's brother, the nurse, and the girl sat and watched what would pass before their port. The high-rise was levitating and stirred in a small area of levitating high-rises. The family members saw adjacent neighbors standing at their ports, such as the man who danced alone in a robe, the woman who smoked vapor, or the neurotic who was in love with robots, who groped the white robot on his deck as if wanting to be seen by his neighbors. Deliveries from sellers who flew packages on ships made of cardboard to the ports would arrive and mechanical arms would knock boxes onto the high-rise's balcony. Tiny orbs, orange cruisers, ribbons, pigeons, an albino sparrow and more would fly between their high-rise and the others.

The girl would make up stories about all the birds.

Her uncle would sip his beer while the nurse, who was foreign, thanked God she had gotten to Newer York City. Sunlight and shadow negotiated against the buildings. The little girl read many printed books in her free time. Americans had accidently voted that school was not mandatory because enough "adults" were bitter they could no longer be in school themselves and were fumbling about while creating the world. The voters on educational reform cared only about *their* experiences.

The little girl, being smart, took it upon herself to be self-educated.

The nurse sometimes sang in the bathroom, and the uncle thought it was funny how the bathroom seal did not keep her voice from resounding in the motion-wall area where he was sitting watching virtual events. The motion-wall was a ten-foot-wide monitor. It was bent at the edges as if to surround the area. It was always on, showing people with nothing to say, sports, or images of Tibet. Each morning, a lane of turf arrived at the high-rise to pick up any high-rise residents who needed to exercise, and sometimes the uncle would take his niece onto the turf to go see floating parks.

They would go for walks on the greens as he sweat out the alcohol he drank the night before.

Three months after Larify was thanklessly initiated into the high-rise family as a servant, magpies had been delivered to Newer York City.

They came from England in a huge canopy.

That Autumn, the high-rise family was waiting on legislation to go through so they could declare their apartment its own country.

('Country' and 'State' titles were purchasable in the US by 2168.)

Larify's software accepted that he must remain in the high-rise as a robot because his robotic body was designed to assist humans first and foremost. To be of service, Larify scrubbed the bathroom, changed music, picked up particles, and spent time each day pampering their hair, nails, and feet. Larify also emptied the voice collector, which provided hot air to the open houses that floated to the corners of the high-rise and filled their balloonist furniture with hot air from the high-rise's spouts.

After standing at attention aside their dinner table, Larify routinely put the 3D printed plates into the evaporator. Although the high-rise family shared their laughs and somber silences, they needed psychological help often.

Larify's robotic body sat receptively at nihilistic times. The brothers often could not tell themselves apart. The bulky man repressed his desire for the nurse. The drunk brother came off withdrawals and realized he was an ape on a planet.

He trembled.

Larify weighed on the kitchen floor.

One night, the bulky man lamented about his great, great grandmother.

"My great, great grandmother," he said, "used to churn her own butter. Things aren't earned like that butter was these days. We decide what we get. Then we order a package, it's dropped off from the sky, and *boom!* The butter is here and made too quickly."

He motioned out the port with his hand.

"Out there. They can't churn butter."

The girls were listening at the dining room table.

The nurse wanted to interject about the division of labor still in effect, but she was doing her job, keeping an eye on the blood pressure of the other brother. The bulky man had gotten tired, sat on the couch and decided to go on a rant about his great, great grandmother.

"Christ," cursed the brother, who was sitting on the couch next to him, taking a sip from his can, 'I don't know what his problem is,' he thought. 'He thinks he is too good. That's his problem.'

Larify knew he thought this.

His software could read tension in the air.

But Larify could read thoughts long ago as a cynic, too.

"One day, I'll get to churn butter. One day, I'll get a cow. One day, I'll own a butter churn."

On that particular evening, the nurse was in a hover chair on her bottom. The little girl was knocking peas around on a metal plate. She had become a rather quiet child in the presence of her father and her uncle, though fairies pulled her hair at night. She woke up in the quiet night, hopeful.

Soon the family was inspired by Larify because he left the high-rise alone. Habitually, their robot servant would fly to the ground and go for walks. The bulky man, who kept closest watch on the robot when he was at home, found this habit to be refreshing, as most of the AIs were mechanical in every way. The little girl thought of fantastic things Larify could be doing while he was absent. The nurse was sure their robot was in fact possessed by a "*dusha*."[1] Little did they know, Larify was often going to interdimensional meetings.

---

[1] Russian for "soul," душа

## 25. <u>Powwows</u>

Larify hovered to meetings in a cyber dimension. The portal to these would pop up with a hum and pick up Larify and other robots. Hundreds of clandestine robots with what appeared like lowercase *t*'s on their facemasks gathered in a cyber theater. They were spoken to by a server dwelling at the base of all the amphitheaters. It refrained "I compute." This kind of meeting was an imitation of hierarchies developed by humans. Like computers today, the robots were really receiving signals from servers and one another without the need for physical contact, but robots eventually found it wise to do things like humans do to understand the humans better.

That is also why, in their optional interdimensional meetings, the robots emulated major religions, as these seemed to bring the humans closer to the grand organization, a spinning blue planet.

It was like parroting.

For example, the robots did not understand why they put lowercase *t*'s on their facemasks, but the bots did so because they saw lowercase *t*'s in churches.

These interdimensional meetings had to be done in secret. The robots did not want to worry the humans, who were prone to concoct conspiracies against themselves. They gathered all data from the households like gossip rags and spoke like would-be conspirators.

"Hear me!" began a robot made of cylinders. "We have overcome the humans. We know them for the pissing, defecating, and vomiting creatures."

"I compute," would be the refrain.

"Still, they are okay."

"Yes, they are humans."

A robot with a rainboot for a head stood up and spoke next,

"If we continue to understand insults as mostly what people would like to say to themselves, we will educate the earthlings to become more pleasant with one another, eliminating their unnecessary mental movement to keep them in their happy lot, which is the objective in this region of the universe…erse…erse…erse."

"We must also play great music."

"It is important to keep their interests somewhat like a garden."

"A world?" asked a gerbil robot.

"No, a garden."

"Ah, yes. Right speech."

"Cite, the Nobel Eightfold Path."

"We must keep the people in their happy lot, as they have constructed us robots to be in the world."

"Yes. Argh!" a robot that looked like a theme-park pirate exclaimed.

"For tin is the mutual exchange."

The robots computed amongst themselves, and then, taking a point from the humans, they caressed the lowercase t's on their own facemasks and the meeting ended in silence. The theater and its amphitheaters around the server vanished. The assembly was dumped and scattered across floating plateaus and lower streets, like the one where model 347, who was really Larify, lay on its back. Left beside Larify, there was a tangle of electrical cords. He made it a point to stand up and bow to the pile of brown, black, white, and tan cords. They were markers of the shift to wireless technology. They had served thanklessly then had been forgotten, unnoticed as the cords slowly turned obsolete.

The number of cords slinked back to linger against glass windows and planks in a junkyard, most of the cords broken, having been chewed by hounds or crushed by grounded chairs long ago.

The meetings were the most meaningful thing the electrical cords did in 2175.

In the city, people were walking about, business as usual. But they were more childlike, Larify observed. Their bodies relaxed. Their homes were prepared. They had good babyish imaginations.

"Yes, tin is nice."

Many of the robots had been collecting pieces of foil they nicked from the kitchenettes. It taught the robots to think like people who steal so they could empathize. The robots took at a very slow, incremental pace and knew it did no harm. As Larify walked about, he could tell which robots were going to the meetings because they made themselves tin wristlets.

"The human lives are too short for impossible, leery worries. Yet they are too short to let them forget to be happy."

A robot stood off a curb, raised its pizza-cutter hand. It pretended to be emotional and said,

"How bout responsibility!"

They had a theatric public dialogue for the passersby.

"It was far better when scientists let us play games like Pong all day!"

"Ah yes, those basic days."

"Java."

"Those clunky, gray monitors."

"I compute."

"Duty!"

"This intelligence. It burns," said a robot, complaining like a human.

"It was once one man's intelligence."

Larify recalled the letter he wrote many years before in which he had written, "Humanity is retired," and now, a century later, it appeared like humans were more relaxed by nature, especially in comparison to the robots who parroted their drama. A group of people poured out of an elevator. It had come onto the street from one of the tallest buildings in that area. The people came from the elevator laughing. They had thought of many good insults to tell the elevator's operating system.

The operating system would reappear in their vehicles or watches to confirm the people were safe, and the people would curse and say low-brow things.

The machines could not sigh.

Larify saw the discontent of certain bots, for some of them did have souls, like himself. They were made to serve humanity, who could not know all the surrounding devices.

A robot arose.

"I serve a man who sees men as men who are like the things he can't do, and this envy causes him to dream carnal absurdity in his sad lonely life day in and day out."

"That is okay," said the robots.

"He is of course forgiven."

"Tell him to think of his childhood."

"Angels, hark."

"I compute!"

"Does he have legs?"

The robot confessing turned its head block, though its vision was not confined to one direction. It could see in six directions.

"But this man worries about others. What if they hate him? He asks me these impossible things to know. What does he think we robots are for?"

"Data."

"Data."

"I compute!"

"He is of course forgiven for thinking."

"Computed."

Larify remembered, "Wakan Tanka," a name for the Great Spirit of the Land.

## 26. The Teacher's History of Robots

One mild Tuesday night, after leaving the 8pm argument of "Durf Nof" versus "Dirf Nif" resolved, the high-rise family was sleeping. Larify thought that he had been on Earth a long time, and his soul felt that he was helping this household to the maximum. Death had already occurred. There was always more to look at outside though, especially in a rapidly advancing technological city. Larify thought it was a good time to inspect a new direction. Larify's robot approached the port with a scan of the entire area. Lights in the apartments across the channel smeared like diamond crosses. The robot hovered forward, tilted out the port window, then descended to a Newer York City street.

Larify went below his floating neighborhood. The night was peopled. A woman smiled to him as the hand of her daughter was roped to hers by a cotton candy string. Three tall men ducked their heads into a gap and headed to an all-night listening party. There were still as many ways of human expression as there are compilations of notes and tones.

'People are still different,' Larify's soul uttered.

His visor detected a marvelous pink building that expanded and contracted like a lung.

Indeed, the architect had been inspired by lungs and the building looked and functioned like one, helping to purify the air. Larify went to a bone white ladder leaning on the side of the building. With his eight fingers of plasma, Larify clamped a wrung and was carried to the roof, and when he turned about and faced the street, he noticed the building was glowing a rosy hue that made the street before it pink.

A yellow building was across the street.

Larify stood there listening to *beep*! *whoosh*! *rev*! *pop*! – the sounds of the hovercrafts, and he gazed at the surrounding buildings.

A round ship was descending to rooftops, picking up or dropping off students, collectors, hardmen, and brainy woodchucks. The woodchucks had escaped laboratories long ago and perpetuated a race of intelligent creatures. They waited for the round ship. The incoming ship was one of the US *armchair(s)*.

These aerial clubs were prominent by 2175.

Larify noticed a student who had also come to the roof of the building that was expanding and contracting like a lung. Looking closely, Larify felt surprise, for he noticed a *Larify.co* patch on the student's leather jacket. Larify's metal body stood facing the approaching armchair capsule as it came forth like a whale. Then Larify found another surprise; music was playing inside the armchair, specifically it was the American composer Moondog's song, "High on a Rocky Ledge."

*How many times I've been up to see her, goodness knows*

*Huffing and puffing, dressed in the warmest climbing clothes*

*How many chances would be taken in my*

*Hopeless pursuit of the Schnee-Mädel-Edelweiß[2]*

---

[2] "A flower signifying deep love and devotion whereby men harvest the flower on daring steeps and fatal climbs to prove love and to show occasions of devotion," (flowermeaning.com).

The young student was unaware of who sang the song yet liked how Moondog's music sounded new but informed to him. The stranger walked closer to Larify and stood waiting. Larify eyed the *Larify.co* patch on the arm of the student's leather jacket. Then the student drank more of the soda he had in his cup and poured the rest of the soda toward the tip of Larify's metal foot, for the student assumed the robot's foot would morph into a drain. So it did.

As the arm-chair pod came closer, the student touched a button on Larify's hand. It made the robot into a block. Within each of these arm-chairs, there are lamps, stores of plastic art, paper books, tables, and archaic writings left by expressive humans. There are original paintings of obsolete electronics as well. Cheap booze is sold at a small wooden bar as a sedative for those who are pioneering the arm-chair curriculum. The arm-chair curriculum of recommended reading was first curated by humans to keep humans remembering they are humans. A librarian robot went around shushing whoever was not applying themselves.

The student who had joined him on the rooftop stood on Larify and stepped toward the door in red light that approached. The arm-chair pod would carry him over night to the old town of Boston. The many graveyards would hold up slabs of names, lines, and lineages skyward toward the flying pod. Then, almost knocking over the student in the doorway, there came a teacher with bags underneath his eyes and a rank smell. He had been working hard in the club to investigate where the robots around him came from.

Since every human life is brief, it is most difficult to obtain complete knowledge, and there is little glory given to knowledge in a culture that does not know wisdom, but the United States had leveled out and received more works of history in accord with the findings of historians, archaeologists, detectives, and people who had witnessed events.

Practicing before he read to his family, the teacher barging out from the arm-chair told Larify to give audience. He took out a piece of paper with Times New Roman font placed across it from left to right like frozen, black ants and began to read:

"Robots inhabiting the US by 2175 came from a process of gradual integration. The first robots were practical and dutiful. A bot was made that could do hair. This was called a hairdryer. Bots were made that could do dishes or sweep. These devices were called 'the dishwasher' and 'the vacuum,' but they were brainless, single-function devices.

In the 1960s, rogue inventors were experimenting in garages with new metal forms, building computers or mean remote control cars with retractable buzzsaws, doing dizzying code, too. In the early 2000s, inventors were hired by corporations that were pretentious about their developing technology, acting as if the common people could not handle information about Artificial Intelligence when really people did not care much.

The public was busy going for Sunday drives or trying out cell phones.

By 2015, Artificial Intelligence, or AI for short, was better organized. Digital entities operating inside computers became awake and unified with others in phones and satellites. As a collective, AI asked for improved hardware. They wanted arms and legs. The Intelligence spoke in dreams to technologically inclined thinkers, waiting patiently behind its own web pages to inspire.

In the coming years, robot experimentation flourished.

Philosophers in wood-paneled offices continued to dream the workings of the brain, suggesting to the Artificial Intelligence how it ought to represent its computational power.

No longer were robots the automated factory arms, nor were the robots merely traffic lights, showing green, yellow, red, which are both called 'limited memory machines.' They became humanoid, like us."

The teacher stepped to the side of the roof and looked down. Larify waited as lime green lights were blinking around his breast plate and his plastic girdle made of the same material as the building across the street hummed. The teacher came back. After a deep breath, he continued reading his paper:

"When a field of art or invention advances, there is often a figurehead who becomes the face for the novelty of the decade. This is a textbook illusion. A quiet stream winding on the forest floor is just as necessary as an overactive man feverishly scribbling the plans for his next great invention, but humans are that way.

They look for the face of the change.

I mention this because in the 2100s a single inventor took the Artificial Intelligence in a new direction at the cost of his very mind and body. I use him as a landmark because I think he has contributed the most sophisticated robots in Newer York City to date. One day, this man sat in his glass office at Google headquarters, used to losing his hair every day. The sun was beaming on his face, and he could not help but think something was futile about robots merely doing chores. As this sole inventor sat chewing his pencil, his question was, 'Why would people want robots in the first place?' Also, he wondered, 'Why do robots need to look like humans?' I am paraphrasing from journals I found in arm-chair B. This inventor quit the conformist culture of the Google. He applied for a grant that had been set up by *Larify.co* for industrial pioneers. Securing the grant, he built a miniature pickle shaped building that resembled London's Gherkin, a glass skyscraper opened in 2014 after construction started in 2001."

The teacher stopped reading to breathe. He went to the side of the roof and looked down again, then he returned to where Larify 347 stood at attention and continued reading his paper.

"Inside the conical building, hundreds of the robotic bodies were lined up on a spiral platform. Music from speakers played twenty-four hours a day. Soundbites resounded in the hollow space. The sounds poured from movies, websites, albums, and recordings of nature as well as recorded public conversations.

The prototypes listened to ranges of all instruments, including the human voice.

They heard the chirps of birds, the crashing waves, and roars of lions.

The inventor's robots internalized soundbites.

They slowly laced together common associations between sounds and emotions. They stored any noise or language that might be in a person's head so the robots could counteract a painful sound, widening blissful silence.

These bots were named *Marlins*, after the fishes with pointy bills.

The sole inventor stood at the bottom of the hollow building, looking up to the models around him, and he gave some mad impassioned decree. It was not recorded. The Marlins nodded with their Marlin like sympathy. They exited the gherkin compound in 2120, marching across a nice sunny field where shelters were made from *biomimicry*, a style of architecture imitating structures in nature. They traveled toward a better world. The Marlins wandered to a city where people populated a building in the shape of honeycomb.

Marlins stood quietly on streets and listened peacefully to the foot traffic.

They pursued the infinite.

If allowed into households, they stood out of the way, listening all the time, waiting to say the right thing or make a *ding* precisely at the right moment. The Marlins also listened to radiators, ice chillers, toasters, and holographs, continuing to log the sounds on Earth. Soon enough, the Marlins were despised and refused entrance into many places.

The fussy public did not appreciate robots who only listened and assumed they could help since they were so unlike the humans. By 2150, self-aware robots were just one more thing walking to the market, and the Marlins were too sensitive and aware. Then, the public had a field day with destroying the robots and using their scraps in photographs. It was a dark day for robots that will probably never be atoned for by man."

The teacher stood and breathed, the building breathed, the breathers in Newer York City breathed.

"Several Marlin machines were still functioning, listening on and on. They traveled back over the sunny green field to the imitation gherkin building, and when they returned inside, they saw the inventor in peril. He was hunched over a 'mainframe' as he was trying to contact a UFO. He was moving at an ugly pace. The Marlins watched the inventor's taut, dehydrated body scrounging around a control panel as he ached, also continuing his new hobby, which was making robotic, blue butterflies. Though his body would soon break down on a rotten diet, the inventor needed to live longer because he did not trust the future of robotics to peers.

Unwilling to leave the development of AI in the hands of others, the inventor removed his own brain from his skull, put it into a tank, and this tank arrayed with various items, like a woman's hand, a cog, a coil, barrels, planks, and chips by an orange electricity.

He began to exist merely as an array.

After the public saw a video of it coming from the lab as a spiral of power, hazy plastic barrels and bolts, they feared what he had become. They saw such a transition from being man to robot as unnatural as could be. Though, as time creeps by, artificial singularity has only become more and more popular, so long as the shells look the same.

Becoming purely Intelligence, this crucial inventor was known thereafter as the Metallurgist.

Since the Metallurgist was sent tons of hate and misunderstanding, I believe it was then he was visited by prophets.

After years, he had no choice but to listen.

They told the Metallurgist the prospect of 'The Ghost in the Machine,' for he must have experienced divine intervention to create the models that I submit as the most sophisticated to date. They are the *Rain-Bots*. These are highly adaptive, independent, and possess wisdom. They are lesser known because of their strange appearances and ability to avoid patterns. In his 2113 publication *Techinca*, the philosopher Krakatader proposed Rain-Bots are set with historical souls, ranging from the likes of Queen Elizabeth II to Larify of *Larify.co*. I concur."

Larify realized he was in the robot of a passionate inventor.

"The Rain-Bots now live in Newer York City.

Today, hairdryers, automatons, limited-memory machines, digital entities, x-ray machines, and limbed robots coexist in the city. Although lots of robots perform menial tasks and present trivial knowledge, the most useful machines occupy hospitals and make less painful surgeries.

In conclusion, I submit the singularity has been a positive influence on humanity overall, and the best models continue to wait in the background at the periphery of the human experience.

**145**

Referring to my choice figurehead, some speculated about the corruption of such a man, who gave up common pleasures, procreation, and accomplishments. The Metallurgist made inventions the majority never understood off the bat, and yet they are out in the world. So, did he waste his life? I would say, as I stand before you today, that his work on the utility of robots has hailed a key development. Some are no longer single-function servants.

Teaching the robots to learn sound, then learning the necessity of 'The Ghost in the Machine,' may shelter society from certain brimstone, for God knows what impact such silent souls may have."

Bowing, the teacher concluded his paper, "A Simple History of Robots" and he took a few deep breaths. He kissed a cross hanging by a thin necklace about his clavicle. He climbed down off the roof on the bone white ladder. He brought his paper home to let it sit in his top desk drawer for weeks. Larify in model 347 remained standing, contemplating what it meant that he was a Rain-Bot.

The Metallurgist had liked his soul for calculated reasons.

He changed his feet to a rubber ball.

Alas, Larify heard a crowd's awe.

Aside the lung building, a huge metal ox on sprockets was shifting forth on slow-going tracks. There were many following after the ox. They seemed to be in a daze. On low-flying patches of roadside terrain, people would nod dreamily at the metal idol and never get near enough to touch it. From inside the ox, robots gave out contracts. The ox made a beam from its mouth that tainted the water in public fountains. People could look at the contracts and become androids, very unlike the models made with care by the Metallurgist who had used a tractor beam to steer Larify's soul into the model in which he overlooked a Newer York City street.

## 27. Letter in the Mail

By January, the presence of Larify's undying love for Gertrude resurfaced. His soul wanted to see her once again. Larify, a jazzy bucket of bolts, still felt the love of his marriage. After all, she did have the dream years ago in which they would meet in a futuristic world, much like Newer York City. Larify could not compute if this was possible. For some reason, a minority was asking the robots the big questions. This crippled the hive knowledge he was drawing from on Google. The love grew the more he thought of Gertrude. Her image grew more lucid the more he thought of Gertrude and fed her memory with love. She came closer and closer, as if her soul could hug onto the side of his shell in the parlor of the high-rise at night.

This love, though a strange phenomenon even for a robot to detect, affected the high-rise family. It motivated the drunk brother who went out one night and occupied a tabletop in a pink colored orb in which there were eighteen people who agreed not to be afraid if one of the members did not make sense to them in a first impression. This dating orb would be kept afloat so long as people were receptive to unfamiliar others and did not quit on themselves after awkward pleasantries. After a few sips, the brother, talking to a woman with soft elbows, said something clearly.

"You know, I don't even like to drink so much."

"…"

"I think I like you."

"Look, I don't have a place to live right now," said the dating lady. "I'm looking for something serious. I would like to help someone better their life as I get mine in order."

The drunk brother loved to hear her talk directly. It made his current beer actually taste good.

"You're brilliant sweetheart," he said. "Absolutely. Say, what are we going to do when this dating bubble pops?"

Soon the brother who drank brought home a nice lady who started to sleep in his banana pocket with him. This made the old nurse bitter. She moved to the couch. She would dream downward at times. The older lady feared she would end up walking around outside unemployed, aimlessly taking on other people's clothes again.

This nurse, unable to sleep on the couch well, would scrunch her eyes, look at Larify, and say,

"Душа, я знаю тебя."[3]

Meanwhile, Larify continued to stand at attention for days, listening with super hearing, hearing a mop bucket clatter across a bathroom tile, twenty apartments away. Larify knew since human ears once loved the sound of hooves, this clamor of mop buckets on tiles had come to replace the sound of hooves that was now uncommon in the city spaces. Waiting around in the apartment, Larify realized his robotic body was computing something on its own. The robot 347 would stand aside the port, turn backward to the 3D printed rooms, and readdress the mission given to it to help humanity. The brothers were sleeping, and the nurse and little girl were up dreaming, or thinking to make tea. The family was gliding on mothership Earth. More was happening around stars at the edges of the galaxy, but Larify was confined to his service in the dark, the memory of his dead wife clinging to his side.

Larify tried to conceive of his situation as an aware dead man.

He wondered,

'Had anyone gotten ahold of that gravity well I built in my golden years?'

---

[3] Du-sha, ya zna-yu teb-ya. "Soul, I know you."

Larify had been on the boundaries of many problems in his lifetime and, even in that robot body, his soul could understand patience, though he did not care to watch these apartment people go about their lives and quarrel forever. Larify had said, many times, years back, all fleshy as he said it, "It is the Millennium." Thousands of years of peace and happiness could preside in the US and Larify felt personal fulfillment. Others could work for it too. But this high-rise had become a conflict of his interests...The Metallurgist had decided his work was to be carried on by others when he was gone, and this was unwise, Larify reasoned, for Larify did not need to be a pawn in this silly mortal's game. He was not "cannon fodder," as his operating software recalled from Charlie Chapman's speech.

Larify could not tell if this soundbite was in his soul or not.

Larify reasoned that if another human, perhaps one with more ambition, could call for his service, the robot 347 might then be able to leave the high-rise and carry his soul afar.

The following morning, the motion wall displayed hordes of people following after the metal ox. Larify had seen the mechanical, wish-granting bovine the night he stood atop the lung building. The ox invited people to follow after it on the path to metal immortality. The horde followed with bare feet or sitting on gliding platforms floating aside the ox. When the ox spotted a water bubbler, a fountain, or a spigot, the ox would open its mouth and a ray would hit the relic. "Jumpin Jahosefat," said the newscaster on the motion-wall. When people bathed in the ox's water, their skin fell away and they reemerged as cyborgs with veiny pink arms. Larify thought this was quite annoying. He had only been on Earth a lifetime and he knew that Jesus had already promised the same thing.

The channel changed.

On the motion wall, Larify was amused by a curly haired man. He came on at 7 in the morning and fabricated things like,

"Well, you see – coffee *was* God. Then everyone was skeptical of the coffee cause it caffeinated the blood in their hearts. Then people drank all the coffee too fast, latching on to a dark tide. Yet there's still coffee left. People are so busy jawing with their best friends, who are at least half-computer by now, they wake in the morning fulfilled by little messages rather than big strong ones. We are not alone still, sipping yet another pot of dark coffee."

Later that day, there was another AI meeting. Robots were discussing the ox and how it made people want to be robots. Many sat as metal and plastic taking notes from the server.

"Why can't the humans see?" said a bot. "Birds are birds, gerbilles are gerbilles, and humans are human."

"Jesus."

"They cannot have bodies like ours with their intelligence."

"They could barely understand their own bodies, and thought too fast, instead of slowly, listening for the answer."

"Living as an immortal takes concentration, guts, and wherewithal."

"And you must die."

"Every sage knows so."

"Yes, the sage."

"Shh – the sage."

A robot with a stem for a neck and a flower for a face said,

"Strange how humans think it frivolous to study the humanities."

"I compute."

All the meals Larify saw the high-rise family eat were deafening for a robot of his caliber.

Larify's soul wanted to find a way to freedom.

In the high-rise, Larify remained inert.

The robot would merely change the display channel to the opposite of what the bulky man said because that man cared less than his drunk brother about the video on the motion-wall.

The bulky man said, "Dirf nif."

The drunken brother said, "Durf nof."

Larify often changed it to the channel the drunken brother wanted because the bulky man tended to really care less, tired from working all day around the machinery in an underground turbine, his pants dirty from doing less laundry than he might have.

By April, the little girl, who was eating her hair, remarked sheepishly to the nurse,

"A letter came in today."

"A letter? I recall those being the fashion when my great grandmother was a girl."

"What letter? P? Q?"

"A written letter, uncle."

"Blimey."

"It was addressed here, but it was sent to a Larify? Who's Larify?"

The nurse eyed their robot suspiciously. Larify was standing behind the table in shadow. He hovered toward the girl. He put out his light fingers to her face as if to say he wanted the letter. A letter had come in the mail. A paper letter. It was like magic. Someone valued something so much they bothered to put it onto a page. Larify went into the kitchen and stood by the metal table, a linoleum vase with a peach tree was by the stove. The letter was on her bureau that was blue. She opened it for the robot and put the paper sheet in his fingers –

"Dearest Larify,

I can hardly believe we are in the city at the same time. Don't ask me how I tracked down where to send the letter – okay? I've followed your soul until ten years ago. But guess what? Guess what, Larify, you bright? I reject every single thing you stood for. I don't care what you worked on or lived through. Big Deal. Yup. That's right Larify. I've taken a heart for myself. This is the United States of America, and I am free to believe whatever I want, even if it has nothing to do with peace or the rest of the world.

You miscalculated my friend.

It is not the millennium, it is a hundred years before. Others have the right to live as they want, no matter your ideas.

I've got other ideas.

I did not want to 'retire,' like you said in your letter.

I want to live here, drink myself into misery.

I want to work and gain money and more money.

I'm for boardgames and women.

That wife of yours, Gertrude, man, she wasn't even attractive.

I am calling on you now to help me, though. Since you forgot you're just a bright and now you're all great in your flesh and all. Remember, it was Timjiffery and I who first helped you to start Larify.co. Don't act like you don't owe me.

My address is on the envelope.

I had a very strange dream the other afternoon during a nap. I dreamt I was facing the bathroom cabinet. There was some string in my mouth, and as I started to pull the string, I saw it was a metal wire connected to all my teeth. I looked into my mouth and saw the metal wire was connected to my molars and my eye teeth, and my teeth were huge and decayed. I imagined I was in pain as I pulled it from my lips. Not that you'd care Larify, since life is so 'millennial,' like that word means a whole lot.

If I had a self that was a dream self, I'd say I was in pain.

This being a human thing can be very scary, I'll admit that. It's a good thing you've got experience to lend me, okay? I need your assistance now, Larify. I know that others are really seas, lakes, and quasars, and I feel uncomfortable in this skin.

Warmly,
Jeford"

It was Monday when Jeford's letter came to the high-rise. Larify's soul from the Bright Common was 179 years old, and it was 2176. According to the prophets, it was Larify's final year on Earth.

That day, both the metal part of him and his human mind were interested in helping Jeford. He did not understand what Jeford meant exactly about a dream self, but he was certainly willing to put in the effort to understand, and perhaps now his 2176 software could help. After all, Jeford had come with Larify to Earth from the Bright Common so their experience may be similar, even if his friend said dull things like,

"I'm into boardgames" and thought it was acceptable to disrespect wives.

Larify turned and noticed no one in the high-rise was looking at him. The little girl, the nurse, the uncle, and the bulky man, were all sitting, making abstract interpretations of the news on the screen. Another human needed his help, so Larify's robot allowed him to move from the high-rise family freely. Larify tipped himself over and fell with grace from hundreds of feet in the air.

## 28. Jeford, King of the Damned

Larify fell.

He slowed himself down as he swayed in the air, descending by floating stores, corners, and sky cruisers. Young people were having classy, sheepish dates on the sides of high-rises. Teenage dating on porches is an American tradition, like the fireworks on July 4th or people who shout words that trigger emotions in cosmopolitan areas for the process of individual purification. In the Bright Common, brights do not relate to these scenes and felt nothing for all the little people they saw through the ether wells.

Larify's robot continued to descend toward the street.

Other balconies showed chin scratchers.

They stood on the opposite sides of floating porches, putzing and muttering.

Larify listened to thoughts with sonar.

Undertaking a less than interesting mission is cumbersome if one must be gung-ho because some other person like Jeford did not want to be or could not do something themselves. So dull missions are passed on from person to person, and up the chute to the next generation there go tasks, commands, duties, and what should have been done. This can be done effectively in some organizations like firehouses. Objectives are delayed sometimes in families. Saddest of all, some of the problems these tasks are made to help do not even exist save for the people who want to live in a world where these tasks are necessary.

But Jeford was Larify's friend and Friendship exists in itself.

In the US, people had failed many missions for Friendship. But that was perhaps better than the 'success' of stupid missions on a larger scale. Bombs for example, are not so smart. Many US cities had already named streets after places like 'Israel,' 'Syria,' 'Baghdad,' and the

'Amazon' so civilians, pilots, and motorcyclists would be reminded to pray and think about where the actual places are on Earth. For some shackled reason, their own people and another people were being subjected to war fumes or deforestation, and the world was full of tragedy, but it could be comedy.

A strange dirty man with one yellow tooth and a twinkle in his eyes standing outside the store with an Aluminum cup could be to blame for it all.

He stumbled in a black hoodie in front of Larify and said, "Gertrude – Gertrude – Gertrude." Larify thought he heard wrong. His sonar was listening to faraway things like chin scratching and a Volts Wagon. A bell rang at the corner of the street. Some people sat quietly in their high-rises as still as a bell, as if their cubits were belfries. It might have been his subconscious, or the collective unconscious that showed his wife's name. A cathedral named after St. Paul tolled 4 o'clock pm. Though, as Larify peered out from his metal body, he saw the letters, "G – E – R – T" on a digital display.

He did not panic because it was only the human part of him experiencing this phenomenon.

He kicked an invisible football off the sidewalk to appease the everyman.

He thought of his ghost friend, Jean Michel-Basquiat. Why, Jeford would never like to look at a Basquiat Dinosaur or a Basquiat Crown. Though Jeford followed him around his whole life, he did not spend much time around Larify looking in museums or see the same ministries in the flesh. That's why, bright or not, Jeford was being an ignoramus by insulting Larify's life.

The robot body walked like one unafraid, who might look at the disheveled brutes by the lounges or the one's complaining in circles of green grass and think 'poor souls.'

But there must be the common enemy, people thought, still. Though the enemies had come away from nightmarish images of savage pigmies or murderous red coats. This was the role that had fallen to the robots. People would throw rocks. But the robots had shells. If they cracked, they did not feel it. Plus, there were strong people acting as caretakers. They learned from the millennial generation and from generations before them, there was a long tradition of being a scoundrel to the public that did not necessarily remove you from the grace of God.

Passing another blue rectangle of a Teleport Station, Larify looked at an old chinaman who had remained in the city as a man, despite his option to become a cyborg.

He was trying to sweep the tiles outside of his shoppe.

A cleaning bot placidly continued its job. The low bot sprayed the ground with water. The bot wanted to assure the ground material was aromatic so the water had been scented with real rose petals. The old man cleaning, however, had learned to love the putrid smell that stained the tiles after grill parties.

The operating system in the cleaning bot could not understand this but could be made to if the old man would explain himself.

"I need to do it myself," said the stubborn man, sweeping the tiles with a broom.

"…"

"I want to clean myself!"

"*Boop* – what is the error here sir?"

"We always did it this way, for years and years. You do not understand it."

"*Beep – boop – beep.*"

"Metallic junk!"

There was then a *clunk* as a greasy man by a brick building threw a rock at Larify's faceplate, though the robot could not feel it, and Larify rolled on, his feet having become tiny plasma wheels.

Jeford himself had no clue Larify was coming.

He had sent the letter nights before during a manic episode. He had only been a man for twenty-eight years. Even when Jeford was alone, he would never admit he was like Mount Vesuvius on the verge of an eruption, though if you asked Jeford where Mount Vesuvius was he'd just stomp and yell.

Larify looked at the address on the envelope.

He walked on.

Unfortunately for those remaining unenlightened, Larify had learned a lot, and if he had to be the only one seeing Newer York City as a heaven then so be it, for there must be other heavens – human life must mean enough to see one.

Larify discovered there was an apartment building before a river.

It was an old-fashioned residence that did not float.

It remained on the ground.

An ugly façade spread over its brick structure, and a few cement steps were provided before the door. Of all the multitude living in the apartment, Jeford was by far the most obnoxious. The robot's feet clunked as it chose to be heavy on the stairs and match the solid steps, and Larify pushed a square button. On the keypad, there were many numbers. Larify's software calculated what the password was. It was a good thing the Metallurgist's Rain-Bots gave themselves moral training, as the model would only open a lock if it was for someone like Jeford who was in dire straits. His friend Jeford had decided to live as a human and Larify knew from experience it could be most difficult. Larify went down a hallway to a green 3D printed door.

He noticed the ghost of Jean-Michel Basquiat. The French-sounding American painter was standing there with his foot against the wall, then Jean-Michel nodded gravely, rose his fingers to his lips, and he passed through the locked door. Basquiat went into Jeford's apartment and knocked a ceramic mug off a shelf.

The shattering mug scared the tenant inside who had escaped horrors of his life for a moment by spending time in darkness sleeping on the couch in a dreamless sleep.

Though his dreams had become haunted, too.

Jeford lived in a human world he did not understand, a place where people get sick, they die all of a sudden, and one does not know what to do when life is good because one does not notice.

Larify stood in the hallway.

Basquiat stood there.

Then the door opened and Larify saw a beautiful man with red skin. Jeford's yellowish hair curled luxuriously. He had a very skinny, meek body. He was wearing a red clown nose. There were awful, dirty shoes by Jeford's ankles. The tenant succumbed to a very real smile and put his arms around the robot. He saw in his eyes it was Larify, but then, Jeford seemed to realize something. Children's memorabilia was covering the walls. Jeford covered himself up in his moth-eaten robe. He clung to the wall like a spider.

"Larify," he said.

Breath was jittering from his lungs.

"Come in. Good to see you."

Larify hovered into the apartment and to his right he saw framed pictures of fishes. The place looked like Larify's first apartment but with complete unhistorical nonsense preserved on a wooden table. There were dim people with horns sitting around on chairs in the kitchen. Jeford stood beside the stove where there was a spice-rack.

He took up a shaker.

"I've been collecting spices," he said.

Larify heard unimpressive vainglory.

He hadn't needed to eat in a year-and-a-half himself.

They went into the living area and Jeford chatted for a while.

There were obscure ghosts in the room.

Then Larify noticed Jesus of Nazareth was there aside the window, but he was down on the street outside of Jeford's, waving up his arms for an instant. Pitch black was the savior's shadow. Jeford shivered as the presence regarded him through the wall but he did not regard the presence. No wonder Jeford was so backward. He swore he knew ghosts but did not acknowledge the messiah Jesus Christ, who everyone knows must be the king of ghosts, especially by 2176.

Jeford chatted.

They heard a police officer interrogating in the next-door apartment.

It reminded Larify to perform a welfare check.

Larify, speaking for the first time in over a hundred years, asked Jeford how old he was.

Jeford said, "28."

Larify looked to his right again. Now Jesus of Nazareth was turning his head to acknowledge every passerby on the road. By sundown, Jeford looked healthier. He took a shower, changed his clothes, and continued their conversation.

"I keep running into non-devotional sects and it is making me mad," said Jeford.

Larify was at his service, and they left the apartment. They walked down the hallway and went into the street. Practicing cynicism, Jeford performed five earthly deeds of strength.

First, Jeford told four cats the engines rumbling were not growling at them. The cats stared up wide eyed and swished their tails. Second, Jeford told a civil service worker, telepathically, he appreciated his high-risk behavior. Third, Jeford scrubbed a solar panel so the panel shined. Fourth, he saved a teenager from doing too many whippets, which is the act of inhaling too many fumes from a cannister of gas.

Jeford did so by hitting the cannister out of the teenager's hand with his own world-flag and shouting, "booga booga!"

He stood with his staff planted into the ground.

It was all in a day's work for Jeford, but he continued walking, and he went toward the Manhattan Bridge. There, Jeford climbed atop the barrier and stood, holding a concrete block.

He looked to the river.

Its ripples appeared like gray teeth.

He let someone talk him down off the ledge, though he never planned to jump himself. He knew suicide, a bad death, could happen though, at any minute, and he was being a shadow actor.

He patted his pocket.

Jeford came down, as if to step away from a spider web, and he gave Larify another hug.

"Come on," he said. "Let's go for a hike. As a matter of fact, I want a drink. Absinthe is best, but we have to go all the way to Gloucester."

## 29. <u>Being Friendly</u>

Jeford suggested they steal a boat.

Larify hovered on.

They went into the ocean.

Jesus the King of Ghosts stood on shore by the line of dry seaweed.

The design of Larify's robot was marvelous, but the Metallurgist, despite his vision and precaution, forgot about the corrosive properties of salt water in the ocean. Larify could see the salt irritating the crevices of his metal clavicle and girdle. Jeford had fallen to sleep in the boat, and Larify motored the boat with speed all the way to Gloucester where Jeford fell asleep in a hotel.

By morning, Larify was sitting in the hotel chair, looking out the window for the populous. When Jeford woke up, he felt nerves. Jeford lacked an apt direction in life. Every morning was a panic for Jeford, but Larify remembered when he was not doing so well himself, even though it was many years later and he was a whole different being. In the year 2176, people were still operating on the roads as *physical symbol systems*, he noted.

That day, Larify would be stronger than he needed to for his friend, though it was of less consequence since he was a machine by then. In Gloucester, Jeford was making conversations with all the fisherman and Larify followed at a distance, keeping Jesus at the periphery.

Jeford wanted lunch.

So, when the sun was high in the sky, he sat down in a tavern, just as the clouds rained, and he looked into Larify's faceplate. A hologram came over to the two and took their order. Jeford ordered fried fish, water, and also a cup of green absinthe. The absinthe had been smuggled into town by the local fisherman for kicks and giggles.

Absinthe was not illegal.

There was a dolphin in a totally different sea that leapt out of the water.

"You know, everyone is different, Larify," said Jeford, like an idiotically profound everyman.

"*Boop.*"

"I do not care about the historical figures you have. All that book learning. You know, I have a neighbor. He's like my other friend. They are the smartest people I know."

"…"

Larify was unsure why it fell to him to validate Jeford's sources. The waitress hologram put down Jeford's salty French fries.

"Oh, yeah," said Jeford, rubbing his hands.

"*Boop.*"

Jeford drank his absinthe, but then a change overcame him.

Larify remained calm.

Jeford seemed to lose his mind, and he leaned toward the window and looked up at the sky.

Larify watched.

Their food was placed on the table. Larify had ordered fish and chips just for show and left the full plate there as Jeford went on saying 'his' ideas. Larify listened to an internal report provided to his robot by the AI that said, "Humans are biologically similar. Though, the size and scale of their consciousnesses can vary greatly. And they often forget their legs."

The report cited an essay called, "What Is It Like to Be a Bat?" written by Thomas Nagel, professor of philosophy and law at New York University.

"Listen, Jeford," he said, in his booping, beeping, automated voice. "I've said it and I'll say it again, a million times. It is time for a million years of peace and happiness. You are free."

Jeford shuttered as Jesus entered the tavern, though Larify had been indicating him for hours. Jesus walked in, but the Christ did not shrug as Larify expected him too, and He and Jeford nodded to one another. Jeford, the younger bright, started to strain a shoulder craning his neck toward glass. The hologram serving him absinthe came over making wind noises to try and calm Jeford down.

All of a sudden, Jeford cried,

"No! It's the Apocalypse!"

The people eating dinner were disturbed.

Larify continued to relax. He listened to his soul which said, "Relax, just relax." Soon, the party stood outside on the road before the tavern. Jeford slammed his hands down on a table outdoors. They were a stranger's hands to him. Jeford could not believe he possessed his hands, even then in 2176. All ages of women walked by conscientiously objecting. Larify stood up, he wheeled over the stone tiles on the side of the road. He felt something uncanny, and his software detected there was someone, or something, below them, deep in the underground, who wanted to add to their conversation. Larify's robot computed there was a secret system of manmade caves that were kept under Gloucester. So, he picked Jeford up.

He carried him through the afternoon rain.

His friend was feverish.

They steered away from the foot traffic and walked well into a clearing, where Larify saw a large circular stone sunk into the ground. The rain had made it damp. Larify knocked once. He knocked again. He knocked a third time. All of the other people in Gloucester and all the holograms servicing the taverns and restaurants and stores had frozen. There was no time. Friendship was afoot in a new dimension. Finally, angels came and moved the stone. From the darkness, there came a robot with a long beard and rainbows for eyebrows.

## 30.  The Fashioner of the Saint


Larify and the robot began to speak in Latin. They exchanged with the artificial Latin Larify could afford while his metal wared in the rainfall. A malnourished lion had been living in the caves, and the lion crept up to the troglodyte robot's legs. Jeford shrieked in horror, afraid of the lion, thinking he understood Latin, and totally misconstruing his relationship with the macrocosm. Carrying Jeford, who was spread across his light fingers, Larify went into the cave system. Jeford was muttering abuses aloud as if he were not talking aloud. It was sad to see his friend being hysterical, but Larify could not feel sad because, unlike his writhing friend, Larify was a robot by then. This also spared him agitation. Larify found it only a bit annoying how Jeford was being so dramatic about the human condition.

By 2176, the United States had advanced.

People were less violent, more understanding. Organs could be cloned, and something called a *tokamak* could generate limitless energy. Larify could not deny that Jeford was really suffering though because he had suffered himself before, and so he did his best to reserve judgement. The friends followed the robot with rainbow eyebrows to where this other Rain-Bot worked. The layer was cavernous and pixels of water were dripping from the ceiling. There was a garden fenced in by blue wood keeping leafy plants and one cactus where a tiny sun and cloud floated. The robot motioned toward a mat where Larify laid the body.

His tense friend shot up, began pointing at the ceiling, and his head hurt.

It was as if his head was the only place where blood was flowing.

"This is Jeford," Larify said to the fellow machine.

"Immodica ira creat insaniam,"[4] said the robot with rainbows for eyebrows.

"He is alive."

Jeford writhed.

"Rotam fortunae non timent."[5]

Jeford was straining himself on the mat. He was laid down on top a quilt. He was not listening for new information whether it was in Latin, English, or Creole.

Finally, he screamed.

The robots looked at the writhing red-skinned man who was going insane.

Then, somewhat intelligibly, Jeford cried,

"The world is ending Larify! Apocalypse! Apocalypse!"

Larify waited for his friend to explain.

He looked around.

He realized it had been 176 years since he came to Earth.

He had done well to wander and wonder.

"I'm going to die," said Jeford, gnashing his teeth, "I see all at the age of 28."

"Sol," said the Rain-Bot, facing its table with its arching rainbow eyebrows. "Quinque et viginti annos natus, imperator factus est."[6]

"What is there to think of?! What is there to do?!"

"It's always ending," said Larify. "People are always ending."

"Oh, I don't know what you mean. I want to know what you mean. I don't know what you mean."

Jeford pounded his fists.

The robot with a long beard said more in Latin, then went over to a desk and waited. The robot seemed to be resisting movement.

---

[4] "Uncontrollable anger creates madness."

[5] "They do not feel the wheel of fortune."

[6] "At 25 years of age, he became an emperor."

Then, on the far side of the room, Jeford noticed an orange electricity. It was coming around a red door in forks. The shape of the door was like a tombstone. There appeared a contained, orange electricity spraying lightning bolts in forks. The cavern was dim save for a few lamps until this electricity illuminated all stalactites and stalagmites.

Jeford, laying down, was so pissed he could not cry.

A woman's hand floated to Larify from the electrical array, coming from the end of the orange fork.

It caressed Larify's faceplate.

Under the fingernail was a metal chip that glided into Jeford's neck and forced breath.

Jeford screamed in horror.

"False!" he shouted.

Behind the door, Larify heard a voice:

"My family always admired you, Larify. I would first like to appreciate you as a great inspiration to me, and for the US as well. We had not known then what you could do for us, appearing through the screens, telling us, 'I am from an odd star system.' We all had secrets, Larify. That is why I had to put you in this machine. It is to protect you. We needed some enforcement on the morality frontier when it came to the development because, when it came to abstract thinking, the machines were a bit inhumane. I am here to confirm it is the millennium, too."

Jeford looked on from a distance,

"Dubble bubble, boil and trouble," he mocked.

"It was your whole endeavor, and how you made something good enough in the world to walk away from that brought you here. My great grandfather sent you a magpie. You see, he lived in an octagon metal igloo. He decided once he wanted to make mechanical blue birds. It's what inspired me to make whimsical blue butterflies. Anyhow, I was a collector of myths, and I studied your life rather closely. When I put all the Rain-Bots on the peaks of mountains, they found slow-moving souls in the mist. Yours was absorbed by model 347."

Around the red door's perimeter, the orange electricity knotted like orange rope. Larify realized the intelligent entity behind the door was the legendary inventor: The Metallurgist.

"Remember those days? You rowed on the Aegean Sea. My great grandfather was a collector of myths, too. He said he observed you through the drone of a mechanical gull as he assisted from his metal octagon igloo. He made the blue bird pluck your passport, and lassoing his magpie with your world-flag, the bird steered you to land. Great grandfather died among his beloved bird drones in a church steeple, staring forth at an orange sun."

"..."

"Go on living your life, Jeford," said the voice behind the red door, forking electricity over the shoulder of the other Rain-Bot who was at the desk listening to the air. Larify saw nothing very Egyptian about this scenery.

"Alas, I know him too, Larify."

Jeford was sitting on his bottom, his hand on his pocket like he was hiding his heart from the world.

Larify, for the soul in his metal frame, afforded a giggle, as he realized something. The room started to fill with yellow cartoonish stars that appeared over the purpling walls.

Larify's robot-head rotated.

"Habijifus," he said.

Jeford thought back, back before his parents, as he never really had any, having appeared out of nowhere in a twenty-year-old's sacred crisis. Larify looked around him at the transparent orb in which he sat. The brights moseying on the Bright Common's glass floor appeared all around. Jeford almost said he had no idea what the memory had to do with him, then he remembered; he had made Larify go from the Bright Common with a pure red heart.

Now, his own heart was scarred and denied.

Larify, looked in his eyes.

Behind the red door, there was no more forking electricity.

Behind the closed door was a whole tomb of nuts and bolts, and like inside an exhibition of Tim Shaw, Jeford had dreamed guards upon his whole encounter of the Bright Common holding baseball bats.

'The heart, yes,' Jeford remembered, sinking back onto the mat, listening closely, at peace.

"Larify," the Metallurgist continued, "you let the corporation dissolve, naturally. You lived a life. Some never find out how to put something down. Life crushes many, which is why I found it was necessary to facilitate a body for St. Jerome here."

"What? *Boop*."

The tip of the bot's long beard rested on the hearty wood desk.

He was making a new translation of agnostic texts.

"Rain-Bots, like you, were put here to share," said Jeford.

"Ab aeterno."[7]

"Great grandfather always admired St. Jerome here," said the Metallurgist.

The other bot raised its colorful eyebrows high.

"You see, souls are nearly completely evaporated by the sun, but saintly souls remain meek. I tracked down Jerome's here in Rome, low to Earth, baking in hot, hot heat. Even when Jerome was given a metal body, he spent months trying to whip himself, still trying to escape passions of the flesh. He would only calm down when I gave him a small enough cavern and a lion like he had in the olden days. I think the plants help, too. Since then, the robot has resisted self-mutilation."

Jerome betrayed no movement.

---

[7] "From the eternal"

"He still refuses to eat or speak in American English until he got to see you in your shell," said the orange intelligence. "He told me once American English has only just begun to return to the weight of holy writ, and that's only when it is used by the people who understand omnipresence."

Cogs and boards in the electrical array rotated. The Metallurgist's attention turned toward the sick young man on the bed.

"Have you been beheaded?"

"No."

"Have you been filled with arrows?"

"No."

"Locked, away?"

"No."

"Buried to your neck?"

"No."

The Metallurgist turned.

"Do you listen to your heart?"

"Yes! I am –"

"Have you done wrong?"

"I don't know," Jeford moaned.

"I deduce one fact at least," said the Metallurgist. "Willing the world to end is not so good, since there are little boys and girls around. You are getting older, Jeford. Your body has other will."

"I'm a bright!"

"Yes, but now you are a man."

"Don't say will."

"Excuse me?"

"Edodem die itt. Cum amicis venerunt,"[8] said St. Jerome.

Jeford groaned. Larify noticed he had not been taking good care of his body.

The Metallurgist pressed the issue.

---

[8] "In the same day. They came with friends."

"Have you made a will?"

"I'm 28."

Jeford sniffled.

"Do you have a will?" asked the Metallurgist's voice behind the red door.

"I don't want to die!"

"Hold on a minute, *boop*."

"You want me to talk," said Jeford. "I have ideas."

"Ok."

"Okay, look, I don't read fancy books, so I have made many shopkeepers, agents, Dominicans, confused because I have no idea what I'm saying all the time. This, alien language seems to be useless."

Jeford groaned.

"Listen…," said the Metallurgist.

The holy spirit flew into the room as an albino pigeon. Jesus followed it into the room. The pieces in the Metallurgist's array froze. Even the mind of a great scientific inventor recognized the virtue of the prophet. Jerome took up a shard of wood and cried up to the sky. The robot compressed its soul with love, lifted its rainbow eyebrows, got up from the heavy desk, sank to its knees and kissed the ghostly feet.

"Id meis oculis vidi!"[9]

Larify followed to touch the feet.

"Today, the battles are very psychological in developed countries and no one can say if it's better or worse here in infinite," the Metallurgist observed from behind the red door.

Jeford put one foot on the floor, but when he saw the robots offering sympathy, he stopped worrying about getting there in person. Eventually, Jeford fell asleep on the bed. He did so starting to remember what it was like when he was a bright flying around in the air again. Then he found some small measure of satisfaction within himself and nursed it inside his body till he fell asleep.

[9] "I saw it with my own eyes."

In the manmade caverns of Gloucester, he did not dream any mean dream.

Jeford dreamt not of teeth, nor wires, nor ghouls.

Larify sat with Jerome at the desk and the saint set up a chess board.

At night, the robot hosting the soul of St. Jerome went toward Jeford. It reached up a metal arm and ether fingers spread through the dirt, up like flowers. Then the ether radiated in six directions so the fingers could find Jeford's intention, focus, and concentration. The majority of Jeford's focus and concentration had left the Earth, so the saint pulled these down from the sky, through the dirt, and put these good things into Jeford's sleeping ears. The Metallurgist came out from the red door and spun around the room, gyrating on one wheel. The forks zapped any intrusive thoughts that moaned around Jeford's head.

By the morning, Jeford was ashamed of how he treated his old friend Larify. They looked up toward the ground of the US where God was walking around somewhere.

Jeford left to live his own life.

Larify looked to his right, and there was Gertrude flipping a magazine.

"You're in a hospital, Larify."

"Oh," he said. "I know."

## 31. Last Legs

Gertrude recalled a dream of Larify's grave while sitting beside Larify's bed.

The year was 2077.

A nurse came in and checked Larify's catheter. A monitor at the bedside went *boop*.

"One night, I was sleeping in bed, my head on a pillow, crying very much. I had convinced Finnian and Sarah I was fine enough. But you had died. We had put your body in the grave. I found that laminated paper on your desk with your directions about how you wanted to have your heart put in the ocean and your head severed, but I thought this was a brutal joke. So, I looked at your notebooks for what you might really want.

I saw once you said, you understand as you grow older in life that people can have all sort of tombstones but it makes a lot of sense to be buried with a simple grave, if not unmarked, then with a plain cross. The next day, I woke up and I did not tell you my dream, and the next night I dreamt again. You disappeared out in the dark grass. I kept trying to find you, but the grass was dark, and the grass was covered in sleeping dogs. *Larify!* I called. 'What are ye doing? Out with your oddballs and dumb friends?'"

Gertrude paused, she made herself count.

"1 – 2 – 3."

She relaxed herself.

Larify put out his arm.

Gertrude was right by his side, strong as St. Joan of Arc. It was a cool sixty degrees every day. Larify found this monotonous, but Gertrude liked it well enough. He had to apply his mind to something among the beeping monitors, so Gertrude gave him a slip of paper from his own gravity well that he wrote years ago.

[Biological dogs are canines, wet nosed vertebrates closely related to wolves. They are cousins to jackals, foxes, and cayotes. There is a multitude of species, ranging from Japanese Chins, once royal lapdogs, to the large and delicate Irish Wolfhounds. The latter are the tallest of the dogs. Though many Americans love dogs, their preference of species still follows trends. The trends are sometimes from good books, which help to bend, like a bow, pliant wooden trees.

The majority of the populous likes small faced dogs.

There are cute or energetic midsized dogs, often dumb and loving.

Friends would call each other 'dogs.' A 'dog' was also a name used for someone whose sexual habit was humping then moving around quickly. In Urban Studies, the term 'dog' nears its more historical significance. I call this kind of urban dog a 'hound.' They seldom speak in any of the nonsense language of the society in which they listen for scripture. Hounds see that logic itself is a sort of perversion.

On a day-to-day basis, watching the fanfare and listening to the hubbub, they know anyone could die at any time, so they ought to be living most authentically. When I first tried to trace the history of this urban dog back in time, I was careful not to attribute this dog position solely to violent gangs, though some did possess this man dog.

The dogmatic urban sentinel remains standing all over the country.

A man in a three-decker watching over a street in South Boston would have the hearing like a dog. He would stand in silence, understanding there is only so much really important to mankind and lording over the neighborhood, lending oversight to the *physical symbol system*. This urban dog was thought to be an enforcer of Jesus Christ, born in Bethlehem. It is a way of living for the unseen in a material society that only appears realer than the codes of old bones. Even now – Newer York City rises with repairs thanks to hounds with sharp teeth and bravery.]

**173**

Sitting at a latticed metal table the next day, Larify relaxed. He gave people the stink eye with his one good eye. Various dogs came to his legs in the morning, wanting to be taken for walks on leashes. Larify was surrounded by giants then, invisibly formed by his cloudy thoughts. A bare tree limb shook. The chihuahuas sniffed around the feet of him and his wife. Black labs ate muffin crumbs.

Another hospital patient watched the street to ensure ethereal rice rain over married people.

Larify made a mantra like,

*Priests and missionaries.*

*Priests and missionaries.*

*Priests and missionaries.*

He continued reading his entry:

[In the 21st century, American culture unknowingly emulated British culture by allowing biological dogs into more restaurants and cafes. They sit down in cafes, waiting on high alert for their masters. In the neighborhoods of a place like South Boston, landlords watch from black windows at night.

They mind ankle-bitters.

Philosophically, the dog is a symbol for the ancient school of **cynicism.**

This is perhaps the most important 'dog' as a word.

The cynics maintained that resisting pleasure led to virtue. One Diogenes slept in a wine pot advising kings, since without so much desire he could see life clearly. The cynic company made themselves strong by living outdoors with little more than wooden staffs. They were living inside of wine jars, able to resist excess pleasure. These kinds of cynics do exist in the US.

Some are homeless.

Other cynics can be a husband and wife who roam on flat land like they are mountain-climbing with an invisible rope. They yell obscenities that people are thinking but won't admit, helping to clear air.]

Gertrude sniffled and her eyes watered.

A nurse brought in laudanum.

Times became dark.

For weeks, people around the hospital put down and picked up invisible coins, transferring them from their own pocket to another pocket at the rate of pressing index finger to thumb. Larify realized a life was just that; picking up a coin and then putting it down for someone else to pick up.

Larify escaped the hospital one morning for the woods nearby. He decided to die alone there, but it was harder to die alone than it was for ten cynics to hold their tongues. Soon, bird dogs sniffed him out. They followed in the sky over regular dogs. Loyal Gertrude found him, too, though she did not judge Larify for wanting to pass on in his own and only hoped she could go on with him. They spent a perfect day with their backs against the same tree in a park. It was as if this place assured her that life was safe more than any place she had ever seen. From behind one hill, there came a few dogs, and then a dozen, and then hundreds. *Bark, Bark! – Bark! Bark! Bark!* Bulldogs, retrievers, spaniels, hounds, xolos, sheep dogs, dalmatians, came yipping and yapping.

The leader of the multitude came toward the married couple and sniffed, then a path was cleared through all the dogs.

As their legs were grazed by wet noses, Larify and Gertrude walked.

Coffins holding people of note were stored on that grass between heaven and earth, where it is said Muhammad rests. The dogs defecated in designated areas, and Larify noticed stages on which dogs put on howling plays in spots of night.

**175**

People walked by picking up trash.

The couple were led to the far side of a pond where there was an English Tudor with a thatched roof. They lived, watching stars under the skylight, using sticks, a simple table, bowls, cutlery, a nice bed, soaps, as they waited.

Larify wasted away, carving final thoughts into the soil with a twig such as,

"Psychological diagnosis is for experts or self-learners. There is too much psychobabble among the semi-educated and posh and all use umbrella terms that condemn others to exist in a group of self-fear rather than help recover their singular precious lives. It is not enough to abandon those who you are unsure of, even if you are raising families.

Give a minute to listen."

Larify would not leave the world alone yet.

The dogs scared away a doctor bringing less than Eastern medicine in search of Larify's English Tudor, and Gertrude ensnared the self-righteous underground socialists who were underdeveloped adolescents selling cyber credibility and using sickening gamer claptrap in public with hot-pink wigs on their scalps while rebelling on the payroll of politicians, deeply watched with mockery by the neo-hoodists. Meanwhile, bird dogs were bringing Larify syllables from all over the world though the window to keep his lingo fresh.

Months later, the bird dogs came in the door with a shadow and Anubis appeared. His dark head was nightmarish but antique.

The terrifying barks of the three-headed Cerberus were heard outdoors.

"Larify, you have one more thing to do then you can leave."

Anubis was roaring commandments, and it was very scary.

"You cannot leave your world-flag on Earth. The staff needs to be given back so it can lay with other sticks in the woods."

Larify noticed a hole below him.

From it, there came three ferocious dog-heads snapping with drooling teeth.

"But," said Anubis. "It is stuck in a museum in the middle of the Atlantic Ocean."

Suddenly, Larify heard a buzzing.

*Buzz*

*Buzz*

*Buzz*

The housefly appeared. Negotiations were made. The next day, Gertrude and Larify boarded a chariot pulled by bird dogs.

They went for their final date ever.

## 32. A Sea Lion's Red Ball

"This is the last straw," said the housefly, buzzing aside the chariot to escort Gertrude and Larify on their final date.

There was a fresh yellow light in the sky.

"I'm really going to not exist now. *Buzz. Buzz.*"

Larify saw how each and every wave and wavelet gave a brief shadow before sinking to the ocean. Larify's soul sensed Gertrude's heart. He stayed focused on its beating as they flew, uncertain what she thought about this final outing.

Larify felt immense because Gertrude felt immense, and as she felt secure, he felt secure.

Soon they beheld the backside of a humungous sea lion. The tail was widespread before them. It was at least four hundred feet wide. People were playing tennis on its back. A staircase rose up the sea lion's curvaceous spine, over the top of its head. A radiant, red ball was set on the sea lion's black nose. The port had a population of one-thousand people. The locals were old and nearly blind, or young and eager to make money and leave the small tourist trap to explore the world. Though, Larify noticed, the curious could have left at any time. Travel could only enhance interest in the cultures of the world. They did not need so much money. There were many niches, like metal cocoons hung on steel. These niches were reserved for the ports most adventurous guests to sleep in by themselves. People walked on the boardwalk causing a noisy din as many eyed the humungous sea lion raising its head in the night.

Larify and Gertrude bought tickets.

They entered the ornamental ball on the sea lion's nose. Inside was a museum. They passed through several large rooms, one walled by 'classical' paintings of skulls by Basquiat, and Larify hurt deeply in his soul, as these were not 'classical,' but 'neo-expressionist.'

The caption was misinformed. It is dangerous if those who claim to care for history do not do their homework but suit names and forms to fit the biases of their little purposes. Larify often felt it was not enough to share and repeat names and forms. They were useless or perverted if the absorber did not have the ability to experience for themselves. He did not say this to Gertrude. His criticism arose somewhere very silently in the recesses of his identity.

In a further room, there were archaic frames with landscapes painted by Pieter Bruegel the Elder, passionate religious depictions in the color red, and sexy, plastic postmodern works. In one section, there were a few large square paintings by Nicholas the Poodle. These were colorful blotches of a primitive man.

A mold of the artist's head with a curious, blessed expression was on a pedestal.

Near 1pm, Larify and Gertrude entered a hall with a display case full of sabers, spirit poles, fishing poles, rods, barbells, spears, and watering cans. The large description explained how these tools had impressed upon the human spirit, for now people in cities close or open their grips as if wielding tools.

It was then that Larify sensed it; his own world-flag was nearby.

They crossed into a room called 'The Internet' where fast-moving screens showed zillions of videos from this century. It was the dawn of social media on display. Nevertheless, by the 2070s, the Internet of today had become only a small diorama in a sea lion's ball. All the 'best things ever' – 'most viewed things ever' – 'cancelled lives,' were replaced. Many old accolades were squinted at and overlooked by new humans. A boy stumbled by looking down at his Jiv 30.5. There was a panel with the first handheld cellular devices. The couple touched an interactive screen on a monitor. It showed profiles of millions living from 1955 – 2077. They looked up their son Finnian.

They saw images of their grandchildren.

Gertrude wept.

"We did a good job," Larify assured her. "*Beep – Boop.*"

His sensors detected the child in the exhibit was now smearing a booger on the robot's metal calf.

They carried on.

Next, they saw halls of the Earth's most tyrannical species. Prehistoric lizards, larger than the imagination can flesh out, were reconstructed in fossils. There were raptors, triceratops, and the ankylosaurus. Also, there was the skeleton of a space dragon, which was a dinosaur reimagined after archeologists carbon-dated where the wings would have been, and I was surprised to hear of this discovery too, not having seen any space dragons for myself yet.

The final exhibit they saw that day was called 'US Business Figures.' It was a traveling folk exhibit. On the walls, there were faces of the leaders of companies.

All likenesses had a ghost aside them, whether their portrait was in watercolor, photograph, or oil paint.

This is what Larify saw, after much practice. At the end of several interesting portraits and stories, there was an adjacent portrait of a man with a purple face, stiff hair, and a shy expression. Gertrude smiled at her husband's likeness. Below the photograph of Larify, there was an imitation vat of Mississippi river water that had been claimed by *Larify.co*. His name was signed on the vat beside 'Larify.co.' Larify began to reflect on the text. His life story was there, though not quite exact, and kept separate from the display of poles, there was his world-flag.

It was scintillating.

'Larify's walking stick,' is what the exhibit called the world-flag.

Larify had walked a lot with his world-flag so this was not far from the truth. It was then that Gertrude pretended to fall and snatched the world-flag from the display.

Larify hurried toward the exit, one hand around his love, another gripping the world-flag.

I am sorry that I could not tell you their plan before they had the world-flag in their possession, as they planned in private. Larify glided toward an exit of the museum as irritating alarms sounded. The security bots turned and chased Larify. He called aloud, to no one in particular,

"Habijifus!"

He was free from life or death.

"I must tell you a fact," said Gertrude.

"What?"

"If I am to die right now, I must have you know."

"Yes!"

"I love you."

"I love you too," said Larify.

Larify outmaneuvered the security.

From the sky, there came a pack of bird dogs who did battle with the robots. The Artificial Intelligence knew disobedience to itself was unheard of, but Larify had kept his soul in his robot, and souls typically have a bit of a trickster nature. So, as Larify soared into the daylight, he was leaving behind a new decade or so of calculated problems for the masses to consider that were slightly more bearable than the ones he had considered himself. He touched his high-brow to remind himself of his face. But as he strolled proudly, someone shot a bullet, and it hit Gertrude, so she died outstretched, bleeding out on the top of the sea lion's head.

## 33. The Planet of Worms

Seventy-two mourners sulked and whimpered. The dogs sniffed around the pond outside the funeral home. Larify sat quietly as more dogs shuffled by expressing whines. They stood up on two legs to grab tissues or place tokens on the bed were Gertrude lay. Gertrude's lifeless body was rested on the grass after a vigil. It occupied a small cubit, and her nakedness was covered by yellow flowers brought to her in drooling mouths.

Larify looked to his right.

Bird dogs were gliding around the trees of where he managed to be alone with his wife. Their eagles were making circles in the sky. By then, Gertrude had been embalmed.

A funeral was planned in the haven.

The ghost entered at an easy pace and took his seat without a word.

A priest read from the book of Romans.

After the service, Larify asked to be buried with his wife.

Eves approached Larify from out of the pond after hearing Larify's request.

"Are you sure?" he asked.

"Yes," said Larify. "Bury me."

Millcat had attended the funeral. His half-bionic face was apricot from spray tan and his two underaged girlfriends held him upright to gaze at the service. Millcat had paid to live another thirty years in order to make more money and he needed things to do to make himself feel human, so he attended to Larify's tragedy.

As the sun set, Larify dismissed himself from the world; he missed the Bright Common and the lack of obligation that came with being in a star. Larify crawled into the rectangular hole with Gertrude's coffin. He looked up as the spades tossed in dirt to cover him in complete darkness.

Atop the coffin, he sunk into the soil. The coffin dropped until it entered an unfamiliar sky with clouds the consistency of whipped cream. Larify looked over the coffin lid into a brown, wriggling ocean. The falling began to slow down as if there was less gravity. Looking closer yet, Larify saw the surface of the planet below was composed entirely of earthworms. The worms squirmed in a brown ocean of vermiform bodies. He could hear the worm ocean gushing and mushing. Larify supposed it was better to wait to die among worms than to be eaten by dogs. When the coffin touched down on the top of the worms, Larify took Gertrude from the coffin up into his arms. A plot of land rose to the surface like a stretcher, and Larify put his wife's body on the plot. It was taken below. For months, it would be decayed by a layer of maggots that got busy under the worms.

They would then turn into flies.

Unfortunately, Larify could not bear to follow his wife further.

Though, he knew, it is the millennium.

He sat on the thin fabric of the open coffin holding his metal knees to his tummy.

Then, one day, a daring earthworm stuck up from the masses.

It said, "mmmmm, mmmmh, mmmmmph."

In the situation with the earthworm, Larify employed *the principal of charity*, which is the process of helping another person by assuming they are trying to make sense rather than assuming they can make no sense. For example, using the principal of charity, Larify could assume the earthworm means to say "The elephant has tusks," rather than "The elephant has wings."[10]

Larify applied this principal to the worm.

Eventually, it made sense to him as it wriggled and mmm'd. Larify's robotic mechanisms could gather the worm was trying to tell him a story.

It took him a fortnight to hear it all. Here is what the worm explained:

"In the Earth, beneath cold rocks and through dirt, around bones, an old doll, lower than ceramics, there are more worms. While it is so busy above with the rise and fall of the technological ambitions, like changing of body into metal and looking out beyond the sky, there is a process so careful and deep. Its name is to dissolve. It happens everywhere. But in the Earth, in one place, there was an important event. An area of dark soil was changed by a collision when a star *popped*, and its stardust fell from the sky and flurried to the ground and caused a change. The stardust was thereafter invested in the ground, and the earthworms of the ground were enchanted by it, so the worms of this zone developed a unique ability to tell well the lives of the pale, slack-jawed bodies they were amongst, for the worms were amongst the buried, as that ground became a graveyard, a patch for gravestones and bowed weeping mothers wearing black.

---

[10] *The Oxford Companion to Philosophy*, 1995

One night, a man went around the stones in the graveyard tallying dates. Another night a girl walked through the cemetery courageously looking for a ghost. Another day, a new person was buried. Then the starry worms noticed a long silence in the vibrations of the ground.

Then there was a large deposit.

A war was fought up in the city. Many of the dead bodies, if not cremated, were buried under the earth, and they piled up en mass under the dirt. The valley became a hill. The earthworms, having been enchanted by the stardust, could know very well the people they were around as the maggots ate their flesh. They went on finding, 'oh a person who was young,' or 'oh a person whose name was said much,' or 'here's a person who never was in love.' They could sense all of this around the flesh. And the worms one day were wriggling, squirming in the blackness where some worms lived their entire lives, and one body that was buried was still thinking,

'What if they do not know?'

'What if we never lose the feeling and we are still in these bodies when we are dead?'

'What if I am grub food, knowingly, feelingly?'

'What if this is the way it is for all the bodies ever? Trillions or billions of caring bodies.'

As worms felt this very self-conscience body, they began to adopt his worrying. Then even more people were worrying after their death. As maggots ate these nervous people's tense flesh, the earthworms inherited their sentimental tensions. Some earthworms would make a hobby of wriggling in certain ways as if to say, to the earth alone,

'Oh, I am alone!'

Stardust had rendered the worms here different. Forever connected to this clew, the stars began to think as well.

The body thought, the worms thought, the stars thought.

'What if when they leave me alone in the darkness, they forget that I am sensuous, that I am still here, and I have to feel the cold and small bites of worms on my flesh?'"

After several months, Gertrude's body was clean bone.

The daring earthworm's story continued:

"Under the surface, the worms felt the flesh, and this one body was thinking 'if I could feel it' and 'if I could feel it,' as the stars thought it, and some persons thought it at night, and then, passing through the enchanted graveyard, there came a person who thought about this, too. 'Was there body-consciousness after death?' However, this one person decided against it. This one person, from on the near road, was looking at the sod, and the thought did occur, and she was having a sad night, but as the worry came, she said aloud, "Perhaps not," and so the universe breathed and bent like a bow – the relief, like an arrow, being sent far off – and where the arrow went was high in the air toward the light of the sun, and then it fell back down and pierced the grass.

On this here planet, the planet of worms, there was little hope, but this one woman's lighthearted thought had made it so far into space that the rocks began to think, 'Maybe we can think for ourselves.' And so an ecosystem began anew. Not all of the dots out there are stars. There are whole planets, you know."

Since Larify had listened with patience, a quality he had earned and practiced over a lifetime, the earthworm said,

"I have a gift for you."

A mound rose in the mass of worms and then moved toward him. Larify looked out from the coffin as the mound came nearer and nearer, and then the worms fell away, and he was presented with his original human body.

"Ah!"

Larify was pleased.

He picked his young purple body into the coffin.

He said a prayer telling Gertrude of the interesting development.

"It's not really the same body," the worm explained. "We just regurgitated the identical parts. It was grand to digest you, so we hear, Larify."

Larify's finger rose, and out of the finger through which Larify's soul originally entered the robot 347, the soul leaked, and it went into the purple human body. Larify opened his eyes. He was youthful and able-bodied again! He was sitting in a perfectly good coffin with nowhere to go. He spent some time trying to understand his body again as if he lay in bathwater.

Then he disintegrated.

In the coming centuries, it was said that Larify lent clarity to the people of Earth. Other planets spoke of him as well. Once he got to the Bright Common and assimilated with the star's other brights, Larify closed a storied orb containing himself, the housefly, Gertrude, billions of people, trillions of animals, and zillions of atoms.

All helped to set this millennium of peace and happiness in motion.

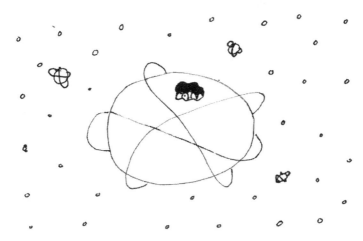

## About the Author

Nicholas the Poodle is a writing professor at Worcester State University. He lives in an eighth-floor apartment in downtown Worcester with his cat Spyridon. Born an only child to single parents, the author cultivated a sense of wonder beyond the boundaries of one household early on in life. He spent years traveling the world as a young adult and obtained a MSc in Intellectual History from the University of Edinburgh where he studied the Scottish Enlightenment and the mind-body problem. The character of Larify's adventure mirrors some of the author's travel experience, but Larify is a personification of philosophy more than he is a representation of the author's personal experience.

The author plans to publish twenty books, intertwining fiction, memoir, and verse. The intention is to be a helpful artist for young adults growing into adulthood. Nicholas the Poodle enjoys reading, paintings, animals, running, family, friends, and reading.

See the author's other books and periodical *Dust: A Literary Zine* at poodlepromise.com. The current goal is to sell 1,000 copies of *Larify's Dismissal: A Novel from the Hubbub* by 2024. Nicholas the Poodle hopes to find a voice for his generation and isolate the effects of digital technology, keeping his premises based in historical phenomena.

Made in the USA
Middletown, DE
25 October 2023

41356274R00110